"Get off the Trail! We've got company!" Rip shouted.

Six riders flashed into view and disappeared quickly around a turn.

"It's Kissick's bunch, boys! Six of 'em! They'll be pilin' into us in a minute or two!"

"Let them come," Rip said tightly. "We'll give them a surprise. Don't bother with the rifles; use your belt guns."

Kissick and his men reached the head of the trail. Their surprise was complete when they suddenly found themselves hemmed in from right and left.

"Stick up your hands!" Rip ordered.

The men raised their hands. Kissick started to follow their example. But then, face to face with Rip, he froze and his hatred swept all reason out of him. His hand slapped his holster, and he fired...

ALSO BY BLISS LOMAX

Sagebrush Bandit
Shadow Mountain
Riders of the Buffalo Grass
The Phantom Corral
*The Lost Buckaroo**
*Last Call for a Gunfighter**

Published by
POPULAR LIBRARY

* forthcoming

BLISS Lomax

THE LAW BUSTERS

POPULAR LIBRARY

An Imprint of Warner Books, Inc.

A Warner Communications Company

POPULAR LIBRARY EDITION

Popular Library® is a registered trademark of Warner Books, Inc.

This Popular Library Edition is published by arrangement with Dodd, Mead & Company, Inc., 79 Madison Avenue, New York, N.Y. 10016

Cover art by Maren

Popular Library books are published by
Warner Books, Inc.
666 Fifth Avenue
New York, N.Y. 10103

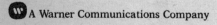 A Warner Communications Company

Printed in the United States of America

First Popular Library Printing: February, 1987

10 9 8 7 6 5 4 3 2 1

CHAPTER 1

It was a raw, blustery April afternoon. Number 7, the east-bound local for Rawlins and Cheyenne, running late, as usual, had just pulled out. The faint ripple of excitement that always attended its arrival and departure faded quickly and Salt Creek settled down to its monotonous existence until the west-bound would pull in, just after five o'clock.

Though it was a U.P. main-line town, which was the only reason for its existence, stockmen along the Sweet Water and in lower Wind River Basin using it as a shipping point, the Overland Limited and the other crack trains never paused to draw breath at Salt Creek. With a scolding toot of the whistle and a blurred shimmer of varnish, they were gone.

Salt Creek no longer minded. By generous count, it had a population of upwards of twelve hundred. Four locals a day was service enough. Someone was always going to or coming from Rawlins, Laramie, or perhaps Green River, to the west. In consequence, Mal Bullard, the sheriff, made it his business to be at the depot to meet the trains.

With the passing of Number 7 this afternoon, he came

riding up the street, the collar of his sheepskin-lined coat turned up against the wind. He was a middle-aged, ruddy-faced man, tall in the saddle and singularly free from worry for one in his official position. But not without reason, for this part of Wyoming had long since settled down to orderly living and save for a little rustling and an occasional blood letting among the Mexican laborers on the railroad, nothing ever happened around Salt Creek to give him any real concern.

With deceiving carelessness Lon Morgan, leaning against one of the uprights that held up the wooden awning in front of the Mint Saloon, observed the sheriff with a keen interest. Inside, standing at the window, his partner, Hank Tovey, was no less concerned.

They had ridden into Salt Creek that morning and tethered their ponies—by design—at the hitch-rack in front of the bank, across the street. By their talk and their looks, they were just a couple of drifting cowpunchers, down on their luck and looking for a job. They were not young men. If their faces were hard-bitten, Wyoming winters had a habit of putting hard lines in a man's face if he had to be abroad without regard for the weather.

Salt Creek had seen their like a thousand times and took them in stride. Bartenders were sympathetic and so was Greek George, the proprietor of the Okay Eating House, where they ate their dinner. But the spring work was almost at hand; this outfit and that were full up; they might try old man Carver, on Owl Creek. Morgan and his partner were grateful, and optimistic; something would turn up; it always had.

A thought ran through Morgan's mind as he observed the sheriff. "He wouldn't be wearin' a sheepskin coat and gloves if he was only goin' to his office," he told himself.

Any doubt of where Mal Bullard was bound was removed a moment later. A man stepped to the edge of the plank sidewalk and hailed the sheriff.

"Hey, Mal, I was just walkin' down to the jail to see you. Ain't you goin' to the office?"

"Wal, I wasn't," the sheriff answered. "I got some papers

to serve on Hog Smith. I figured I'd git out there and back before dark. What's on yore mind, Clem?"

"Why, that shindig for the new officers of the lodge. We got to make some arrangements."

"Look me up about four o'clock," Bullard called back. "I'll be in by then."

Lon Morgan built himself a cigarette and stood there smoking it reflectively, his eyes on the retreating figure of the sheriff. Sure at last that there would be no turning back, he beckoned for his partner to join him.

"We get a break, Mike," he said. "His nibs won't be back till four o'clock."

Tovey, dark and saturnine, nodded woodenly. "I heard him . . . This will be as good a time as any."

"I reckon," Morgan muttered.

Unhurried, they sauntered across the street, the wind kicking up little puffs of dust under their boots. As they reached the opposite sidewalk, a local expressman drove up in his light dray and stopped in front of the bank. This was an unexpected hazard. Morgan and Tovey exchanged a quick glance and pretended to turn to their ponies.

The expressman struggled with a wooden box. He caught the two men regarding him with a seemingly casual interest.

"Purty heavy," he declared. "Box full of ledgers, I reckon."

"Suppose we give you a hand," Morgan volunteered. "We'll carry it in for you."

The offer was accepted. With the expressman holding the door open, Morgan and Tovey walked into the bank.

"John, here's your box," the old expressman called to the owner of the bank, who stood behind the counter that divided the room. A swinging door gave access to the area behind the counter, where the safe was protected by a steel grillwork partition. A door in the grillwork stood open.

Morgan and Tovey took this all in at a glance.

Two of the bank's customers stood talking to John Hume. All unsuspicious, Banker Hume turned to his cashier and said, "Tell them where you want the box put, Richard."

The cashier unlocked the swinging door and said, "You can put it right here by the cage."

Things happened then—swiftly and unexpectedly. Guns appeared in the hands of Lon Morgan and Hank Tovey.

"Git your hands up!" Morgan ordered. "Stand put and you won't git hurt!"

Tovey produced a canvas sack. Into it he scooped the gold and paper currency in the cashier's cage and was helping himself to what he could find in the safe, when a man stepped into the bank, saw the upraised hands of John Hume and the others and grasped the situation in a flash. Morgan could have shot him down before the man bolted back through the door, but a shot that would arouse the town was not likely to help matters. Instead, he barked a quick order at Tovey to get moving.

Holding Hume and the others at bay, they backed to the door. The man who had walked into the holdup had raced to the hotel, on the opposite corner. Tovey and Morgan saw armed men converging on the bank, but they kept their heads.

"You four, turn around and face the rear of the bank," Morgan ordered. "Stand that way till you hear us gittin' away. We'll kill the man that tries to throw a gun on us."

Hume and his cashier obliged (the bank was insured against robbery by a well-known bonding company) but Jeff Hartman, one of the two customers who had been caught at the counter, had other ideas. His money was in John Hume's bank, for one thing, and for another, he had a perfectly good .44 on his hip and it was his belief that he still knew how to use it. When he heard the bandits open the door, he drew and spun around in one motion. It was fast work, but not fast enough; Morgan doubled him up with a slug in the belly before he could fire.

A dozen men, all armed, were running up from the direction of the hotel as Tovey and Morgan swung into the saddle. With a coolness born of long experience, the two bandits sat there and emptied their guns at them. The crowd scattered. They were brave men, but it occurred to them that it was not their bank that was being robbed.

Whipping their rifles out of their saddle boots, Tovey and Morgan raked their ponies with the spurs and flashed down the street in a hail of lead. As is usually the case at such a moment, the shooting was atrociously bad, and they swept across the railroad tracks and out of town without receiving a scratch.

In the bank, Jeff Hartman still clutching his stomach, had breathed his last. Hume ran out into the street, yelling, "Bullard! Mal Bullard! Where in God's name is he?"

Clem Evans came running to tell Hume and the others that Mal was on his way to Hog Smith's ranch and wouldn't be back for hours.

Doc Merriweather hurried inside, hoping he could do something for Jeff Hartman. He came out shaking his head and told them Jeff was dead.

"We don't have to wait for Mal," Clem said. "My horse is down the street. I'll get a rifle. How many of you are ready to go after those birds?"

A dozen hands were raised.

"All right," Clem declared. "Meet me here in five minutes—armed. They're headin' out into the desert. They'll leave a trail we can follow."

The killing of Hartman, long a popular man around Salt Creek, supplied them with a personal interest in capturing the two bandits, and it was a determined posse that swept out of town under Clem Evans' leadership.

Word was sent to the sheriff. It brought him pounding back to town. The looting of the bank and the killing of Jeff Hartman presented Bullard with a serious situation that was not helped any by the fact that the job had obviously been accomplished by old hands at the business. After getting the details of the robbery from Hume, he asked him and several others, who could recognize the bandits, to step down to his office. There, he thumbed over a heavy file of "wanted" notices on the chance that he could turn up a picture of the two men.

"There you are!" Hume declared, a few minutes later. "The

two of them!" He turned to the others for confirmation and got it.

"Lon Morgan and Hank Tovey," the sheriff growled. "Wanted for heistin' a bank at Pulver, Idaho!" He read the information on the circular aloud. "Records a yard long on both of 'em! Half a dozen aliases!"

"It wasn't up to you to spot 'em," said Frank Mulvey, the druggist. "You got a hundred notices in that old file. No man can expect you to carry all those faces around in your mind."

Bullard shook his head. "I missed a trick; I shoulda put the finger on 'em. They were here all mornin'. They looked to me like a couple of grubline punchers. That was my mistake . . . A good man killed and nine thousand dollars gone! I'll go after 'em. I'll send some wires first."

With the help of the U.P. agent, he telegraphed news of the robbery and the names and descriptions of the wanted men to sheriffs and peace officers throughout the State and along the northern tier of counties in Colorado and Utah. That accomplished, he left town accompanied by Buckskin Joe Miller, a dried up little man, now past eighty, but who had been an excellent tracker at one time.

Though the wind had been at work on the trail the posse left, the two men followed it easily enough. An hour's riding brought them to a small desert ranch at Mud Springs. All they were able to learn was that Clem Evans and his posse had stopped there briefly and reported they were having trouble following the bandits' trail.

Bullard and Buckskin Joe overhauled the posse several miles south of the ranch and rode with them until dark. It was apparent to all that there was no point in continuing the search until morning. Bullard thanked Clem and the men and sent home, cold and weary from their fruitless errand; he and his tracker spent the night at the Mud Springs ranch.

Three days passed before the sheriff and Buckskin Joe Rogers returned to Salt Creek. Returned empty-handed. They had scoured the country south of Salt Creek from Bryant Mountain as far east as the Coal Hills. Lon Morgan and Hank Tovey had apparently disappeared into thin air. The only

explanation Mal Bullard had for it was that the bandits had cut back to the railroad and grabbed a freight. It was his hope that when he reached his office he would find a telegram from some sheriff along the line informing him that he had taken the two men into custody.

Only disappointment awaited him. There were requests for further detailed information regarding the bandits; that was all. Unkempt, red-eyed, Bullard walked up the street to the bank without bothering to stop at the barbershop.

He found John Hume seated at his desk with a stranger. "What luck?" Hume inquired, a certain coolness in his tone that had never been there before.

The sheriff shook his head hopelessly. "No luck at all."

"I feared that would be the case." Hume nodded gloomily and turned to the man at his desk. "Mr. Greenwood, this is Sheriff Bullard . . . Mr. Greenwood has come out from Cheyenne," he explained for the sheriff's benefit. "He represents the bonding company that holds the policy on the bank."

Greenwood, a thin-lipped, cold-eyed little man, acknowledged the introduction with a jerk of his head. "I appreciate what you've done, Sheriff," he began. (There was little in his tone to suggest any feeling of appreciation.) "The important thing at the moment is that Morgan and Tovey are still at large. We have secured good photographs of them. Several thousand reward notices are being sent out. The company is offering a thousand dollars for their capture. Of course, I'll be glad to hear anything you have to say. But it might be just as well if we let it go until this afternoon; we are putting a couple well-known detectives on the case. They're due here on Number 7."

"Detectives, eh?" Bullard queried resentfully. "Pinkertons?"

"No, Rainbow Ripley and his partner George Gibbs. They've worked for us before and have always given a good account of themselves. We were fortunate enough to catch them no further away than Black Forks."

"Ripley and Grumpy Gibbs, the range detectives," Bullard

said rather disparagingly. "I know 'em. I knew 'em when they was punchin' cows for Judge Carver's Bar 7 outfit."

"They've come a long way since then," Greenwood said thinly. "They've cracked some big cases. It'll cost us a pretty penny to turn this matter over to them. But if we want to stay in business, we've got to regard one bank robbery the same as another, no matter how little or how much is stolen. Let this pair of bandits get away with the nine thousand dollars they got here and it will only encourage them, or someone else, to hit us somewhere else and very likely make off with three or four times that amount . . . I can see that calling in a couple well-known detectives has rubbed you the wrong way. There's no reason for you to feel that we're going over your head."

"No?" Mal queried, his mouth taking an angry set. "This job has put me under the gun. I figgered I rated a chance to see what I could do about it before outsiders was brought in. If you got other ideas, that's yore business. Let 'em catch yore crooks for you; I'll play my own cards."

"Mal, that's no attitude to take," John Hume declared indignantly. "Under the circumstances, I should think you'd be glad to have a couple trained men to work with you. After all, it's a fact that Morgan and Tovey were here in Salt Creek all morning. You saw them around town. If you'd had your eyes open, you'd have grabbed them."

"I expected to have that said behind my back but not thrown up to my face, especially by you!" Mal's mouth was rocky and he was thoroughly angry now. "If every sheriff and town marshal in the state of Wyomin' grabbed every crook that showed his face, crime would be put down over night. I never guaranteed any man who voted for me that I could recognize a bank robber on sight."

"You took an oath to do your duty," the banker flared back, his glasses slipping off his nose in his excitement. "Folks had a right to expect you to be on the job when you were needed, instead of ten miles away, serving papers in a piddling water suit!"

Mal thought he had him now; John Hume was chairman

of the board of county commissioners and a consistent advocate of economy, whatever the issue. "Damn yore hide, you know why it was up to me to serve them papers on Hog Smith!" he roared. "For four years I been askin' you commissioners for a paid part-time deputy! Every time I brought it up, you knocked it down. County couldn't afford it, you said! Wal, by grab, yo're payin' for it now; I'd a been here if I'd had someone to do my legwork!"

"Gentlemen! Please!" Greenwood protested as the sheriff shook his fist across the desk at Hume. Mal waved him aside.

"There's just one thing more I want to tell you, John Hume!" he bellowed. "You made a crack about me not keepin' my eyes open. Why didn't you keep yore's open? You had a sawed-off shotgun under the counter where you was standin'. Talk about keepin' yore eyes open! You all but invited that pair to clean out yore bank . . . 'Tell them where you want the box put, Richard'—this with withering mockery. "By grab, you'll never live that down in a million years! Salt Crick will be laughin' at you long after it's forgotten all about me!"

Angry as a hornet, he stormed out. Greenwood gazed after him with a pained expression.

"The hotheaded fool!" Hume protested. "I shouldn't have lost my temper with him—not that he'd be any help to your men."

"I'm sure they wouldn't agree to that," Greenwood said pointedly. "I'll see Bullard after he's had time to cool off. We've got a pair of outlaws on the loose, Mr. Hume; if we have to eat crow to get Bullard's help in apprehending them, we'll eat it."

CHAPTER 2

THOUGH LAW enforcement officers and agencies in a dozen Western states had long since come to regard them as a formidable pair of man-hunters, and their continuing success in their chosen field had rewarded them handsomely in a financial way, their fellow passengers on Number 7 this afternoon failed to recognize the tall, lean-faced man with the wide shoulders and keen gray eyes and his pint-size partner, twice his age, as Rainbow Ripley and George (Grumpy) Gibbs, the well-known "cowboy" detectives.

At the depot in Green River, they had secured a newspaper that carried an account of the bank robbery at Salt Creek. Prior to that, their knowledge of the robbery had been limited to what they had learned from Ferris Greenwood's telegram, requesting them to come to Salt Creek at once, if they were at liberty to take the case. Over Grumpy's objections, Rainbow had wired back that they would be there on Number 7. After reading the newspaper story, the little man was still of the opinion that rounding up a pair of small-time bank bandits would not prove either profitable or interesting.

"Chances are we'll lose out on a big job in takin' this case," he declared, bringing the matter up again as they neared Salt Creek. "It's jest a matter of goin' out and gittin' 'em. No detective work required."

"Maybe not," said Ripley, "but the Inter-Mountain Bonding and Surety Company has given us a lot of work in the past, and when we needed it. We owe Greenwood something. We tripped up this fellow Lon Morgan in that Wells Fargo case, out in Nevada. He was sent up for five years. Even with time off for good conduct, he hasn't been out of Carson very long. Does this other one—Hank Tovey—stir any memory in your mind?"

"Never heard of him," Grumpy muttered. "Likely as not, he's jest graduated from the Carson pen, too."

He put on his gold-rimmed spectacles and took another look at the pictured likeness of Tovey. Though the years were piling up on him and his face was grizzled and crisscrossed with wrinkles, the little man was still as tough as bullhide.

"Tough lookin' gent," he observed. "They're mean when their eyes are as close set as that. Morgan wouldn't win no beauty contest either...Robbery and murder." Grumpy shook his head. "I reckon the notice the company sends out will state as usual that these men are armed and will resist arrest. Why do they waste printers' ink on such dang fool talk?"

Rainbow smiled. "I wouldn't know, Grump. Why don't you ask Greenwood? Maybe he could get one of his bright young men in the Cheyenne offices to think up something better."

The brakeman put his head in at the rear door of the smoker and yelled: "Salt Crick! Next station Salt Crick!"

Grumpy glanced at his watch. "Jest about on time."

They got up and walked to the door as the train slowed. Their range clothes, rifles and riding gear were in the baggage car.

Through a window, the little man ran his eye over the group of men and women—no more than a dozen in all—waiting on the depot platform. In the tall, ruddy-faced man

standing at the waiting room door, he recognized Sheriff Mal
Bullard. He nudged Rainbow.

"There's Bullard out there, Rip. I told you I've heard he
was still wearin' the badge over here."

"I see him," Rainbow remarked. "Wonder if he'll remember us."

"He'll remember us all right. That ain't sayin' he'll be
glad to see us; he may feel we're treadin' on his toes."

Rainbow refused to be disturbed; they had seldom found
themselves working at cross purposes with local officers for
long.

"Mal knew us when—" Grumpy persisted. "He may figger
we've got a little too big for our britches."

Rip shrugged. "It won't take us long to show him we
haven't. Let's go!"

Greenwood had calmed Bullard's ruffled feelings by as-
suring him that nothing would be done without his knowledge
and approval unless the man-hunt moved beyond his jurisdiction, and that his cooperation would not go unrewarded.

Bullard recognized the partners as they stepped down from
the train and jerked a greeting. "Been a long spell since I
saw you boys," he said. "I been hearin' about you from time
to time. You look as sassy as ever, Grumpy. Ain't it about
time you called it a day?"

"Shucks, no! I'm jest gittin' my second wind, Mal. I figger
I'm good for another forty years."

"Don't let him fool you," said Rip. "Any time a job comes
along that promises to have a lot of riding in it, he does his
best to get me to turn it down. He wanted me to wire Greenwood that we weren't available . . . You look about the same."

"I am—least I feel the same," Bullard declared, beginning
to thaw. "How are things around Black Forks?"

"They haven't changed much since you left. Cap Weir is
still running his Ten in a Circle outfit. Some of your old side
kicks are still forking broncs for him."

"I'd like to sit down and shoot the breeze with 'em," the
sheriff said. "Reckon that's yore stuff that Ed's wheelin' into

the baggage room. You want to tote it up town with you now?"

"No, we'll pick it up later," Rainbow told him. "Greenwood didn't come down with you, eh?"

"He's busy at the bank. He said he'd come down to my office as soon as he got through. Kinda burned me up when I heard he'd called you boys in. The way this job broke sorta puts me behind the eight ball. Hume, the president of the bank, has been shootin' his mouth off. The two birds who heisted the bank were around town all morning on the day of the robbery. I saw 'em and never tumbled to what the game was. I had to leave town and they proceeded to git busy."

"You've been out looking for them, of course," said Rainbow.

"I went out that afternoon. I been out ever since. Had a good tracker with me. We didn't git back till a few hours ago. I can't say we had much luck. It's been blowin' like hell here for a couple days. Still, we had their trail and we managed to stick with it till evenin', when they used the old blanket trick to break it."

"Which way did they seem to be headin', Mal?" Grumpy inquired.

"About as straight south as they could make it, for twenty miles or more. They struck off to the southwest then, And soon after that they broke their trail."

"Wal, you can be dang shore that's the one way they ain't goin'," the little man declared. "If it was, they'd have dragged their blanket before they turned off. That was jest a slick trick to give you the idea they was goin' to follow the Little Snake River down into Routt County, Colorado, and go over the Vermillion Bluffs to Brown's Park."

"They didn't fool nobody with that nonsense. Brown's Park is all washed up as an outlaw hangout. But as I was tellin' you, I didn't like the idea of you fellas, or anyone else, bein' called in till I'd had a chance to see what I could do about roundin' up Morgan and Tovey. I felt different about it after Greenwood sat down with me for half an hour and talked it over. He guarantees me it won't be a case of you fellas goin' in one direction and me in another. I don't give a damn about the glory of snaggin' those gents, but I do want to be reelected this fall."

"We couldn't do much without your help," Rip informed him. "We're coming in cold; we'll have to depend on your knowledge of the country. Suppose we walk up to your office and sit down and talk things over."

Bullard led the way and they fell in step with him. His office, in a corner of the county jail, was as battered and cheerless as a hundred others the partners had known. A large map of the county, heavily pencilled with notations, occupied the greater part of one wall.

"Suppose you show us what country you covered while you were out," Rip suggested, as he walked over to the map.

With his finger, the sheriff traced the trail he and Buckskin Joe Miller had followed. "Here is where they turned off to the southwest," he explained. "This is all broken country— sand, sagebrush and nothin' much else. If they swung back to the east, they took their time doin' it. Figgerin' it was a feint, I cut down across the alkali flats to the south, thinkin' I might pick up their trail. Nothin' doin'."

"No towns down that way?" Grumpy spoke up.

"A couple places that don't show on the map," Bullard told him. "Just wide places in the road, so to speak, with a store; nothin' more. Some sheep ranches. That's tough country, if you don't know it; you don't find water everywhere. That's what beats me; those birds are either smarter than I figger they are or they're just plumb crazy, headin' for the line. They can git across; but that won't take 'em nowheres; they will git tangled up in the Elk Mountains."

They sat down and discussed the possibilities at length. Finally, Rip said, "We've got a cold trail to pick up. That means we've got to play the odds. The best way to begin is by ruling out all of this long shot speculation and sticking with the few things we know and what we're agreed they most likely have done. We can miss them that way, but it's a chance we've got to take."

"I agree with that," Bullard said. "Where do we begin?"

"I think we can forgit all about the railroad; if they'd got out of the country that way, their broncs would have turned up and you'd have heard about it by now."

"They could have killed the hosses and rolled 'em into a canyon, somewheres," the sheriff argued.

Grumpy shook his head. "I don't believe it, Mal. They're smart enough to know it would be dangerous to show up along the U.P. They'll stay away from telegraph lines. If you want my hunch, I'll give it to you; I believe somebody's taken them in."

"A confederate, you mean?"

"Not necessarily; they more likely showed up somewheres and jumped some party and forced him to take 'em in. You can be dang shore they ain't wanderin' around the Red Desert without grub."

"I'll go along with that." Rainbow looked to Bullard. The latter nodded.

"And I figger we can discount the chance that they turned back north and are headin' across Wyomin'," the little man continued. "They're smart enough to put two and two together; they know you've alerted the whole State and they couldn't git far without bein' seen and recognized. They might run into snow, too; it ain't too late for it."

"Any one of those reasons would be enough to convince me that you're right," said Rip. "But I can think of a couple that are even better. This robbery was a Wyoming job. Like all crooks, Morgan and Tovey will feel safer if they put a stateline behind them. They've got money to spend now. They'll want to put it into circulation. There's half a dozen mining towns in Colorado that are booming right now—gambling, girls and hell in general. You know the saying about Creede—'It's day all day in the daytime and there is no night in Creede.' Creede would be just about their dish—lawless crooks moving in from as far away as California and Nevada. That pair may be in Colorado already. If they are not, they'll be Colorado-bound unless we dig them out before they make a run for it."

"There ain't so many places where they could be hidin' out," Bullard observed, after some thought. "How do you boys want to go about this?"

"If it's all right with you," the tall man replied, "we'll light out of here tomorrow morning and make a beeline for Bagleys Crossing and make our headquarters there for a few days."

"That's purty far east," Bullard told him.

"It is," Rip agreed. "But if I'm right and they've got Colorado on their minds, that's the way they'll go. If we're lucky enough to get there ahead of them, it wouldn't surprise me if they rode right into our hands."

The low grade coal that was strip mined around Bagleys, kept the town going. For years there had been talk of building a railroad from Laramie down through the Medicine Bow Mountains that would open up the country and bring in capital to develop the mines. That was still in the talking stage, and Bagleys' only contact with the outside world was still by stagecoach and freighting teams.

It was Rainbow's idea that word of the robbery had not had time to reach Bagleys—a factor that was sure to be considered by the bandits. Having nothing to fear, they would not hesitate to show themselves there.

"I don't know how you feel about it, Mal, but workin' out of Bagleys strikes me as bein' the sensible thing to do," said Grumpy. "If there's any news of 'em waitin' for us, it shore will be bad news. It couldn't be anythin' else but that they have slipped through. On the other hand, if they're still holed up at some cabin or sheep camp, we'll be in front of 'em. That'll give us a chance to dig them out or cut them off when they try to git through."

"All right," Mal Bullard agreed, "we'll play it that way. I've got some good broncs in my corral. If we pull away no later than six o'clock, we can be in Bagleys late tomorrow night."

Greenwood came in as they sat there. He shook hands with the partners. "I'm glad you were able to get here so quickly. This robbery was carried out in old-time wild west style. Have the three of you worked out anything?"

Rainbow told him what they proposed doing.

"Sounds all right to me," Greenwood said. "I'm leaving everything in your hands. I'll be back in Cheyenne tomorrow. If you have to get in touch with me for any reason, wire me there . . . Do you want to go up to the bank and hear what Hume has to say?"

"Grumpy and I will go up," Rip replied. "Bullard has supplied us with all the facts. Hume can hardly add anything of value to what we know." He turned to the sheriff. "I don't intend to discuss our plans with him. If he's got anything to say, I'm willing to listen. There's no reason why you shouldn't come along, Mal."

Bullard shook his head in an emphatic no. "I've heard enough out of him! If he's got anythin' to say to me, he can come here and say it!"

As Rainbow expected, nothing came of the interview with the banker. They were leaving, when Hume said, "I'm far more interested in seeing those men captured and brought to justice for killing Jeff Hartman than for robbing this bank. I know you gentlemen are recognized experts in your line. Have you made any plans?"

"We plan to go after 'em," Grumpy said pointedly. "I reckon that covers everythin'."

CHAPTER 3

THE PARTNERS left Salt Creek shortly after daylight with Bullard. The cold, raw wind that had been pelting southern Wyoming for days had blown itself out and the day turned surprisingly mild for late April. After they passed the Mud Springs ranch, they found themselves moving across a vast, rolling, sagebrush-covered plain that stretched out before them in long, uninteresting miles.

Measuring the endurance of their tough, grain-fed ponies against the distance they had to go, they held the animals down to a steady, comfortable lope. When they pulled up at noon for a cold snack, they had not put more than thirty-five miles behind them. Along the horizon to the south, a mountain range, snow-capped in places, reared its spiny backbone.

"The San Cristobals," Bullard explained. "Or mebbe you boys know without my tellin' you."

Rainbow nodded. "Been some years since we saw them last. As I remember it, this country changes some before we hit Bagleys Crossing."

"It changes a bit," Bullard said. "Pinches up a little—low

hills and less sand and some grass. We'll hit a sheep camp in about ten miles. A fella named Pat Miles. He's all right. We'll stop for a minute and question him; if he knows anythin', he'll come through with it."

After he had eaten a bite, Grumpy produced his tobacco and smoked a pipeful. "Bagleys grown any, Mal?"

"Not much. Couple hundred, I reckon. Mostly foreigners—Poles and hunkies of one sort or another, workin' the strip mines. We don't have to bother with them; we can g:t the information we want from Aleck Cameron. He runs the general store now and is postmaster." Bullard glanced at his watch. "Mebbe we better be movin'; it'll be nine o'clock or thereabouts before we reach the Crossin'."

They stopped briefly at the sheep camp without learning anything. Soon after, the country began to change perceptibly, as the sheriff had said. By early evening, the Coal Hills were in evidence on the horizon.

"Dust in the air, over there to the east," Rip observed.

"The road from Rawlins to Bagleys," Bullard informed him. "The Friday down stage must just have passed. We'll save time if we cut over to the road and follow it in."

The moon was up before they caught their first glimpse of the lights in Bagleys. Even by moonlight it was an ugly one-street town, boasting several stores and saloons, dingy, a fourth-rate hotel and the cabins of the men who worked in the coal fields. Unlike a cow-town, Bagleys went to bed early. Cameron's store was still open, however, and there was a little group of loungers gathered under its wooden awning. Bullard and the partners left their horses at the hitchrack. When they turned to enter the store they found Cameron in the doorway.

"I figgered we'd be seein' yuh, Mal!" he called to the sheriff. "The stage jest got in with the Rawlins papers and this flier addressed to the postmaster." He waved one of the reward notices Greenwood had sent out. "Too bad yuh didn't git in a bit sooner. Morgan was here in the store a couple hours ago. Bought cartridges and some grub. I recognized his picture soon as I laid eyes on it."

The little group that had been lounging in front of the store moved closer. One of them stepped up to the sheriff and said, "That's right, Mal; it was that fella Morgan, sure enough! I was in the store, talkin' to Aleck, when he comes in. I didn't know who he was, but he was a mighty tough lookin' gent. I didn't take my eyes off him."

Bullard recognized the speaker. "Did you notice which way he went, Gabe?"

"I did, for a fact. He walked across the road to the Eagle saloon. He wasn't in there long. Hennig was behind the bar. He says Morgan had a drink and bought a couple bottles of whiskey. When he comes out, he gits on his horse and jogs south. Reckon his pardner was waitin' for him somewheres along the crick."

He was referring to Bagleys Creek, since it was the only one in twenty miles of town.

"Looks like you called the turn, Ripley," Bullard growled. He did not attempt to conceal his annoyance; he could have been in Bagleys two days ago, had he so elected.

"Don't let it throw you," Grumpy advised. "I warned you if we got any news here it would be bad. It could be a lot worse. We've picked up three days on 'em; we ain't far behind 'em now."

They moved into the store and the sheriff introduced the partners to the proprietor. The latter suggested organizing a posse.

"No, go after Morgan and Tovey with a posse and they'll run," said Rip. "Chances are they've camped along the creek for the night. If that's the case, we've got till daylight to locate them ... What did Morgan have to say, Aleck?"

"He didn't have much of anythin' to say. He told me what he wanted and I set it out on the counter. He did ask me how far it was to the Colorado line. I told him we called it fifteen miles. Reckon it's a little more."

"Was he surprised?" Grumpy questioned.

"Not a bit. He said that was about what he figgered."

The little man nodded. "He was speakin' the truth; either him or his side-kick have been in this country before. They wouldn't have come this way if they didn't know what they were doin'. Morgan was jest checkin' up; he wanted to be shore they could slip across the line in a couple hours. But they won't do it tonight; they'll have a good look-see by daylight before they put Wyomin' behind 'em. We'll find them camped down the crick eight, ten miles."

Bullard, stung by the realization that a few miles more would take the bandits beyond his jurisdiction, was all for going on at once. Rainbow saw no point in it.

"If they kept on moving, they're gone, Mal. If they're still on the creek, we'll run into them by daylight. Our horses are weary. It won't do a bit of harm to feed and water them and let them rest for an hour. I wouldn't mind having something to eat myself. I don't suppose we can get anything in Bagleys this time of night."

"I'll make some coffee for yuh and set yuh down to beans and bacon, at least," Aleck offered. "I'll have Gabe lead yore broncs around to my barn and take care of 'em."

He was a bachelor and had his living quarters at the rear of the store. It did not take him long to prepare an appetizing supper. Bullard recovered his temper as they ate.

"How well do you know the creek?" Grumpy inquired.

"I been up and down it a couple times, but I wouldn't say I know it."

"It would help some if we had a man with us who does," Rip spoke up, sensing what the little man had in mind. "There can't be too many good camping places."

"Yuh better ask Gabe Bouchard to go with yuh," said Aleck. "The Frenchman knows every foot of Bagleys Crick. Shall I call him in?"

"If it's okay with Mal."

The sheriff nodded his agreement. "It's a good idea. We want to play this as carefully as we can."

Gabe expressed his willingness to accompany them.

"I want to warn you," Rip told him, "that Morgan and Tovey are wanted for murder as well as bank robbery. They'll put up a fight if given a chance. That means gunfire."

Gabe Bouchard expressed his contempt for the danger

involved with an eloquent shrug. "I git my horse and rifle. Give me ten minutes. If they're camped on the crick, I'll find them; I know all the good spots, some on one side, some on the other."

"Then you're the man we want," Rip told him. "You don't have to hurry; if we pull out by ten o'clock, that'll be early enough."

It had been a long time since anything had happened to stir Bagleys Crossing out of the doldrums. Word that Sheriff Bullard, accompanied by two detectives, had reached town spread like wildfire and when coupled with the fact that one of the bandits who had robbed the Salt Creek bank had been seen there earlier in the evening, it produced a sensation. Men who had been about to retire for the night pulled on their britches and hurried down to Aleck Cameron's store. By the time the partners, Bullard and Gabe Bouchard were ready to leave, fully half a hundred were gathered out in front. A number offered to accompany the sheriff.

Bullard spoke to the crowd. After declining the proffered assistance, he said, "It might not be a bad idea for some of you to git yore guns and spend the night down at the Crossin', jest in case those birds break back this way. I'll ask you to boss that job, Aleck."

Just outside of town, Rainbow called a halt. "We better settle a thing or two right now. We'll have to split up; Grump and I will take one side of the creek, you and Gabe will have to take the other, Mal. It's the only way we can be sure we don't miss them. If you spot them, drop back and get word to us. Don't try to close in on them alone. We'll do the same if we locate them. Are we set on that, Mal?"

"Certainly! That's the only way to play it. I want to take that pair alive. If they know the crick at all, they most likely forded it right here. You can't put a horse across any place you please; she runs too deep and fast for that."

"They had to know the country to git this far without bein' spotted, didn't they?" Grumpy queried. "We better take it for granted that they know what they're doin'. Gabe says most of the good camp grounds are on the west side of the stream. That ought to settle the question."

"There's somethin' else that needs settlin'," Bullard observed. "How we goin' to keep in touch with you fellas, and vice versa? There's places where the bottoms widen out and are purty well wooded."

"Suppose we give you and Gabe a twenty minute start," Rip suggested. "That'll keep us behind you and you'll know where to look for us. I don't have to tell you, Mal, that Morgan and his pal will be quick on the trigger. At the first sign you get of them, stop where you are and send Gabe back to find us. We'll play it just as carefully on our side of the creek. If I have to get across to you, I'll find a way."

Bullard and Bouchard forded the creek and were soon out of sight. Twenty minutes later the partners began moving down the eastern fringe of the bottoms. Save for the growling of the mountain stream as it tumbled over the rocks, the night was still. Though the moonlight was bright, the shadows in among the willow brakes were black and impenetrable.

Grumpy rode in the lead, hunched forward in his saddle, stiffly alert as he searched out the darkness with his puckered eyes. Rainbow was equally vigilant. Several times they moved in across little grassy flats that took them to the water's edge. Men had camped there at times—there was bountiful evidence of it—but there was no one there tonight.

Their intentness and the slow pace they were forced to pursue, began to wear on them. An hour and more had passed when the little man pulled up and waited for Rip to join him.

"What do you think?" he muttered. "I figger we've come a good four miles."

"All of that," said Rip. "It still leaves us some room. No reason to be discouraged yet."

Midnight passed. Hope was dimming, when suddenly gunfire racketed across the night—a shot, and then a flurry of shooting. It came from further down the creek, possibly half a mile in advance of the partners.

The pattern of the shooting told them nothing. The night

was still again for a few minutes, and then they heard the swift running of ponies.

"There they go!" Grumpy growled. "Bullard jumped 'em! The dang fool didn't wait for us!"

"Listen!" Rainbow commanded. And then, "That's Gabe, riding back and yelling to us."

It took them a few minutes to find a spot where they could safely ford the creek. They were no sooner across than Bouchard thundered up to them, so excited he had difficulty telling them what had happened.

Grumpy took a firm hand with him, "For cripes sake, stop yammerin' like that! One thing at a time Gabe! How did that shootin' start?"

"We moved around a bend and was right on top of them— no more'n fifty yards from their fire. It had burned down to coals, but we could see them fellas stretched out asleep. Their ponies was grazing beyond the fire. I figgered we'd turn back and Mal would send me lookin' for you. Instead he said, 'No, we got 'em where we want 'em and we're goin' to grab 'em.'"

"I'll say that was shootin' square with us!" Grumpy rapped sarcastically.

Rainbow only urged Bouchard to continue.

"Before we could move, their ponies scented us and started whinnyin'. Them two gents rolled away from the fire quicker'n you can say Jack Robinson! Mal charged in, yellin' for 'em to throw up their hands. The dang fool caught a slug through the shoulder first shot. The second knocked him out of the saddle. I had my gun buckin' by then, but the way the lead was singin' around my ears convinced me it was time to run."

Grumpy was ready to explode. Rip checked him. "No point in blowing off steam," said he. "Bullard saw a chance to cover himself with glory and he couldn't resist it. If he hadn't gone back on his word, we might have grabbed that pair tonight . . . Lead the way, Gabe; we'll see what shape he's in."

They found Bullard conscious but bleeding freely from

two wounds in his right shoulder. "—I made a damn fool play. I—"

"Don't waste your breath crying over spilled milk," Rainbow snapped. "Lie still till I have a look at you."

He asked Bouchard to pull up some dead sage and build up the fire. When that was done, he cut Bullard's shirt away and examined the wounds.

"They're too high to be serious," Grumpy muttered, as he bent over the sheriff. "Neither one hit the lung."

He ripped up the shirt and went to the creek and wetted a piece. With it, Rip washed away the blood that covered Bullard's chest and shoulder. Both wounds continued to bleed.

"Is there a doctor in Bagleys?" he inquired of Bouchard.

"Yes, Doc Streeter. You want me to go for him?"

"Gabe—can you get a wagon in here?"

"Shore! I been haulin' firewood out of these bottoms for years."

"Well, get the doctor and your wagon." the tall man ordered. "Get back as quickly as you can make it. In the meantime, we'll make Mal as comfortable as we can."

"You don't have to do all this fussin' over me," Bullard protested. "Set me on my horse; I can make it back to town."

"And bleed to death on the way?" Rip's tone was curt. "You'll stay right where you are."

Continued applications of ice-cold water from the creek checked the bleeding. Grumpy finally sat down by the fire and puffed his stubby pipe. His lined face reflected his weariness.

"Why don't you stretch out and doze till they get here?" Rip asked.

"No," the little man answered. "I'll stick it out. It'll be comin' on to daylight by the time we git back to Bagleys. We ain't goin' to overhaul them law busters tomorrow or the next day; we better sleep till noon. We'll need a pack horse and a camp outfit; no tellin' how long we'll be knockin' around Colorado."

"No telling is right," Rainbow responded soberly.

Bullard started to speak. Rip tried to stop him but the

sheriff would not be silenced. "You boys are welcome to my horses. Why don't you take them and git after those birds? Don't let 'em git away from you. I'll be all right here till Gabe and the doctor come."

"No," Rip said emphatically. "You had your chance, Mal; we're playing it our way now."

CHAPTER 4

"As LONG as Mal says for yuh to use his hosses, yuh better take him up on it," Aleck Cameron told the partners. "They're better'n yuh could buy around here. Lord knows Mal won't be needin' 'em for some time to come."

It was mid-morning, and Rainbow and Grumpy were in the store, buying blankets, grub and a sketchy camp outfit. They had just come from the hotel, where Bullard was resting comfortably. On the doctor's advice, he was to remain there for another day before being taken back to Salt Creek.

"The only reason I hesitate," said Rip, "is because I don't know when we can get them back to him. It might be never."

"We can always send him a check," Grumpy countered. "I been runnin' around town lookin' for horses. I agree with Aleck; there ain't a good one in town."

"All right, that settles it," the tall man agreed, with a smile.

"You set out our stuff, Aleck, and we'll pick it up in a few minutes and be on our way. I want to have a word or two with Gabe Bouchard before we pull out. Send him around to the barn when he shows up."

They had their pack made and were lashing it down before Bouchard joined them. "I wish I was goin' with you," he declared. "But I reckon it might be some time before I saw the Crossin' ag'in."

"I'm afraid it might," Rip agreed. "We wanted to ask you a question or two, Gabe. Will we have anything ahead of us between Bagleys and the line?"

"Not a thing—that's if you mean to turn off the crick at what we call the Elbow and go over Crazy Woman Pass."

"How can we be sure to know when we reach the Elbow?" Rip questioned further.

"You can't miss it; the crick almost doubles back on itself. You start bearin' off to the southeast when you leave it. It's a long climb to the Pass but it ain't a stiff one. When you git over it, you'll have the Painted Meadows country open ahead of you. About thirty miles down that way you'll hit Lively. There's cow outfits down there; plenty of 'em. Reckon that's where those skunks we run into last night are headed for. They can catch the narrow gauge Thunder River and Northern at Lively and git out of northern Colorado in a hurry."

"That's our guess," Grumpy acknowledged. "We know the lower end of Painted Meadows. Mebbe we can hit Lively in time to head 'em off."

"You'll see a cabin or two after you git over the Pass," Gabe told them. "There'll be mountains all around you. That's one thing in yore favor; once a man gits into the Meadows, there's only two ways he can git out; that's to come back this way or head for Lively."

After saying goodby to Bullard, the partners jogged down to the Crossing and began descending the creek.

"By grab, we're on our own at last!" the little one muttered thoughtfully. "If we make any mistakes now, they'll be our own mistakes!"

They found the Elbow without difficulty. By mid-afternoon they were climbing over Crazy Woman Pass and into Colorado. Before they were through it, a snow squall struck them, a wild, spring storm that lasted for an hour. If Morgan and Tovey had left any sign of their passing, it was covered now.

"We got to go it blind," Grumpy complained, teeth chattering as the blast struck him. "They're either ahead of us or we've missed 'em completely."

"We've got our eggs all in one basket," Rip agreed. "But it's not a bad gamble. You don't believe they stuck to the ridge and are going to fight their way through the Medicine Bows into North Park, do you?"

"There's a railroad over there."

"And it'll take them back to Laramie." The tall man dismissed the suggestion with a shake of his head. "That's not the direction they want to go, Grump. Snow up here. Chances are it's raining down in the Meadows. That'll slow them up some; and when they hit ranch country, Morgan will be smart enough to keep to the hills and try to avoid being seen. That may give us time to pull ahead of them."

They ran out of the snow, only to have a cold rain pelt them. The short afternoon was drawing to a close when they caught sight of a hillside cabin. They turned that way, hoping to get some information regarding the quarry.

A couple of jaded broncs stood forlorn in a pole corral. There was no sign of livestock nor any evidence that a plow had ever broken the virgin sod around the cabin.

"Reckon he's doin' a little minin'," Grumpy observed. "Got a hole in the ground somewheres."

The trail of wood smoke that was being whipped away from the chimney by the wind said that whoever lived here was at home.

The partners tied their horses to the corral gate and walked through the rain to the cabin. A hairy old man, stringy and weatherbeaten opened the door. He looked them over suspiciously. There was a strong odor of whiskey on his breath.

"We were just passing," Rip told him. "Your cabin looked good to us. Mind if we stop in for a minute?"

"No, come in! Can't offer yuh a drink; I jest polished off the last I had." A cadaverous-looking pointer tried to crowd past him. "Git back thar!" he cried, giving the dog a boot. It retreated to the fireplace and hunkered down.

"Fire feels good," said Grumpy. "Snowin' up in the Pass."

"I figgered it wuz," the old man declared. "On yore way down from Bagleys, eh?"

"Yeh," the little one admitted. He was a past master at drawing a stranger out and at the same time divulging no more than he deemed advisable. "My name's Gibbs—George Gibbs. This is my pardner, Rainbow Ripley."

Watching the old-timer carefully, he saw, as he had surmised, that the names meant nothing to the man.

"I'm Jim Wheelock," the latter responded. "If yo're goin' to sit, yuh better git out of them slickers and dry off."

The partners accepted his hospitality without further ado.

"Must git a mite lonely for you, perched up here above the Meadows," said Grumpy.

"Yeh," Wheelock replied, his faded eyes as guileless as ever. "Yo're the first fellas I seen in months."

"Of course you can always git down to Lively when you have the inclination," the little man remarked, with a chuckle as he picked up the empty bottle that stood on the table. Without seeming to, he examined it carefully. "You shore drained her dry, Jim. Too bad we ain't got a bottle in our pack."

"By gum, that's a fact!" Wheelock declared dryly. "Yuh boys are shore travelin' light, not a bottle on yuh. Yuh oughta see the way some of them Denver hunters show up here in the fall fer me to guide 'em up in the San Cristobals. About all they pack in is a toothbrush and a case of Old Crow."

Rainbow listened with an expressionless face, wondering where all this was leading but convinced that Grumpy had got hold of something.

"So you do some guidin', eh?" the little man pursued. "Not seein' any livestock around, I figgered mebbe you had a glory hole somewheres and was doin' some minin'."

"Ain't no mineral around here," Wheelock informed him. "Every square foot of country has bin gone over. Yet as soon as the weather turns mild, some fool will be pokin' around up in back of me, lookin' for metal." He wiped his unkempt beard with a horny hand and gave Grumpy a shrewd glance. "Is that the direction yore stick is pointin'?"

"No, we ain't out prospectin'; we got a little business in Lively," the little one answered without hesitation. "We hear the town ain't what she used to be."

"By hickory, I'll say she ain't! Lively ain't lively no more. The gold excitement on Moran Mountain has petered out. The last time I was in town, I heerd there wa'n't a wheel turnin'."

Grumpy pretended to be surprised. "I don't like to hear that. How long ago were you in Lively?"

"Late Fall. I—"

The little man exchanged a quick, warning glance with Rip.

"Jim, yo're lyin'. That whiskey bottle gives you dead away. The serial number on the revenue stamp says it didn't leave the distillery more'n sixty days ago. Yet you claim we're the first men you seen in months and that you haven't been in town since Fall. . . . Where did that bottle of Old Crow come from? Did it drop out of the sky?"

The bluff worked; the serial number on the bottle was meaningless to Grumpy, but Wheelock didn't know it. He hemmed and hawed and let his glance wander to the rifles on the wall rack.

"By damn, it ain't up to me to say whar I git my likker!" he jerked out angrily. His tone aroused the dog and it growled at the strangers.

"I'll change yore mind about that," Grumpy drove on. "You got a couple broncs in yore corral wearin' a Wyomin' brand. You know what the penalty is for havin' stolen stock in yore possession." He and Rip had no evidence that the broncs had been stolen, but it seemed a safe surmise. It had a marked effect on Jim Wheelock.

"You better come through," Rainbow advised. "You had company no later than this morning." He pulled out a reward dodger and spread it on the table. "Do you recognize these men?"

The old man was ready to spring back from where he sat and try to reach a rifle. Grumpy pushed him down on his chair. To Rip, he said, "Tell him who we are."

Wheelock lost his truculence when he learned that they were detectives.

"Those men are not only wanted for robbery and murder in Salt Creek, but last night on Bagleys Creek, they shot down the sheriff in resisting arrest. Under law, you become an accomplice by concealing evidence regarding them. Unless you tell us what you know, Wheelock, you'll find yourself in hot water."

"All right, I'll tell yuh! They wuz here this mornin'. They come in friendly like and then poked a gun at me. They wanted breakfast and my broncs. I had to do as they said. They had the Old Crow. They took a drink or two and left the bottle on the table fer me, along with a twenty-dollar gold piece. They warned me to keep my mouth shut. I figgered I better."

"When did they show up?"

"It was early. Mebbe seven o'clock."

"They say anything about where they were heading?"

"Nope. But I watched 'em when they left. They wuz linin' out fer the Meadows."

"All right," Rainbow told him, satisfied that they had got the truth at last. "There's a price on them, dead or alive. If they show up again, you can take that into consideration."

"A thousand dollars, eh? I could use that money." The old man sounded relieved. "I didn't know who yuh was. If yuh'd said, I wouldn't have tried to hold back anythin' on yuh. By the way, do I git to keep that gold piece?"

"You can, as far as we're concerned," Rip answered. "How far will we have to go before we hit the first ranches?"

"Twenty-five miles, more or less. Yuh won't find no roads till yuh git down to Joe Corbett's Triangle Cross. Them fellas is far ahead of yuh. If they wa'n't stopped, they made Lively by noon."

"They won't ride in free and easy," Grumpy remarked.

"Link Easter was warned by telegraph to be on the lookout for 'em a few hours after they stuck up the bank."

"If he wuz, that ole law dog will nab 'em shore enough," Wheelock averred. "Yuh goin' on tonight?"

"We'll go a piece," said Rip. "Rain's about over. Is there an evening train out of Lively?"

"No, jest one mixed train a day. Leaves in the mornin'. The Thunder River and Northern is in bankruptcy. Jest a pile of junk."

The old man came out and watched them ride away.

"He's a cagey old devil," Grumpy grumbled. "That nonsense about serial number on the bottle made him talk turkey. We couldn't have got a better break. We know we ain't goin' by guesswork now."

"We know they're in the Painted Meadows, and that's all to the good," Rainbow returned. "But I was doing some wishful thinking when I said Link Easter would be waiting to grab them. If he got the idea that they might be coming his way, he'd try to plug the smell end of the funnel. Link must be seventy if he's a day, but he's still a capable officer."

Grumpy nodded. "Link's still got his wits about him, I reckon. He was a big help to us when we was roundin' up the gang that wrecked Calumet Consolidated. Night will be on us in half an hour. How far you figgerin' to go before we call it a day?"

"The rain's over," said Rip. "We'll pull up as soon as we find wood for a fire and cook supper. We had only a couple hours' sleep last night, but I think it would be foolish not to go on. We can be in Lively before midnight."

"And what good will that do us?" Grumpy demanded with a touch of asperity. "The town will be locked up tighter than a drum. Lively's best days are behind her; she ain't no rip snortin' cow town."

"It's worth the effort," Rainbow insisted. "We missed our men at Bagleys by a few hours and again last night through Bullard's foolishness; we don't miss them a third time." He turned in his saddle and gave Grumpy a long glance. "You had about all you can stand for one day?"

"Hellsfire, I ain't thinkin' of myself!" the little man snorted. "Look at these broncs! It must be a hundred miles from Salt Crick to Lively. A hundred miles in forty hours! That's askin' too much of horseflesh, considerin' the country we've come over since leavin' the Crossin'. Looks like a crick ahead of us. We'll find a place out of the wind and let these animals rest up for three or four hours. All we want to do is be in Lively before that mixed train pulls out in the mornin', ain't it?"

"Yeh," Rainbow agreed. The little man's scolding told him plainly enough that he was as weary as the ponies.

"Wal, we'll be there!"

CHAPTER 5

IT WAS so early that Lively's main street was deserted, when the partners rode in. When they had seen it last, Lively was booming; the new gold camp of Chipeta, on Moran Mountain, enriching it with sudden and undreamed of prosperity. Empty houses and boarded-up saloons said plainly enough that those days were gone.

"Some change," Grumpy declared. "Reckon our friend Wheelock was right; Lively ain't lively no more."

"Still a good solid town," Rainbow commented. "We'll ride down to the depot; there may be somebody around."

The mixed train, consisting of a little diamond stack engine, combination passenger coach and a single freight car, stood on the track. The fireman, a young, broad-shouldered man, was on the engine, getting up steam. Rip hailed him.

"What time do you pull out?" he inquired.

The fireman turned, seeing them for the first time, and sized them up carefully. "We're due out at seven-thirty-five."

"That gives us over an hour," Grumpy announced. "Where can a man git breakfast at this time of the mornin'?"

35

"The hotel's about the only place. The dining room opens up at six-thirty."

The partners thanked him and turned back up the street.

"He shore gave us a good lookin' over," the little one observed.

Rip nodded. "I noticed. Not a bad sign."

"Meanin' that Link's passed the word to be on the lookout for strangers?"

"I'd like to think so. There's the hotel; we'll just leave our horses at the rack after breakfast and see if we can't find the sheriff."

The dining room was just opening when they stepped into the hotel office. A girl showed them to a table. She was pretty, and the fact did not go unnoticed by Rainbow.

She rattled off the menu, regarding them with interest meanwhile. The tall man caught her at it.

"No, we're not the fellows whose pictures you've been looking at in the post office for the past few days," he said, with a grin.

"I see you're not," she answered banteringly. "I wouldn't call either one of them good-looking."

Grumpy frowned. "You can bring me some prunes and ham and eggs. If the coffee is ready, bring it in with the prunes."

"You can make that for two," said Rip. "By the way what time of the morning does Sheriff Easter get down?"

"He usually goes by about this time," the waitress answered. She took a step or two to the window and looked up the street. "He's coming now. You want to see him?"

"Yeh, just tap on the window."

The waitress got the sheriff's attention and beckoned for him to come in.

Link stood in the doorway a moment later, a spry, clean-shaven little man who did not look his seventy-two years. From under his white, hooded brows, he levelled his glance at the partners and his eyes began to twinkle with pleased surprise.

"Come in!" Rip called. "Don't stand there making faces at us!"

"By Joe, what do you know?" Link exclaimed. "I shore wasn't expectin' to see you boys!"

He hurried up to the table and pumped hands with the partners.

"You look as chipper as ever, Link," said Grumpy.

"I'm feelin' fine," was the hearty answer. "Don't tell me it's that trouble up at Salt Crick that's got you down here."

"You guessed it," Rip replied. "We left Bagleys yesterday noon and came over Crazy Woman Pass. A few minutes ago, we were down at the depot. The fireman was getting up steam. He gave us a careful looking over, Link. We thought maybe that could be traced back to you."

"Mebbe so," Link told them. "When I got Bullard's wire, I knew it was the regulation message, but I figgered those birds might head this way. I haven't seen anything of them. But I can tell you for a fact that they ain't gone through Lively; I've watched every train out. Done some ridin' too. No word of 'em. You boys got any reason to think they're this side of the Pass?"

"They've been in the Painted Meadows since about eight yesterday mornin', Link," said Grumpy.

"No question about it," Rainbow seconded. "We missed them by a few hours at the Crossing the other evening and again a few hours later on Bagleys Creek... Sit down and have some breakfast with us."

"I'll have a cup of coffee; I jest put away a big breakfast."

While the waitress was in the kitchen, Rip told Link what had happened on the creek.

"A fool play, shore enough!" the old man declared. "You picked up sign of them after you came over the Pass?"

"You know Jim Wheelock's cabin?"

"Naturally."

"They stopped there, took his broncs and left him a bottle of whiskey. We had a little trouble getting Wheelock to talk."

It called for further explanation. Grumpy supplied it.

"No question about it, they're in the Meadows," old Link

acknowledged. "They may show this mornin'. Git yore breakfast and we'll go down to the depot."

The girl brought in the prunes and coffee.

"Rip, has that pair any reason to believe you boys are
chasin' 'em?" It was a pertinent question.

"I don't think they even know Grump and I are on the
case. That being so, I suppose you're asking yourself why
they didn't ride into town yesterday."

Link Easter nodded thoughtfully. "That's exactly what I'm
askin' myself. The only explanation that occurs to me is that
somebody tipped them off that I was watchin' for 'em to
come through. Some cowpuncher could have told them."

"And they could have been told that you've got only one
train a day out of Lively now," said Grumpy. "They might
figger it'd be safer to show up jest in time to catch it. It'll
be time enough to worry about what's become of them if we
don't see 'em at the depot."

Several other early diners came in. The three men lowered
their voices against being overheard. Breakfast eaten, they
walked back to the depot. The train crew, fireman, engineer
and conductor, and several townspeople were on hand.

The ticket office was open. Inside, a girl, still in her early
twenties, was in charge. There was a business-like air about
her, and though she wore no makeup and her starched waist
and tweed skirt were plain and rather mannish, she was un-
commonly attractive. She wore her red hair pulled back from
her face and caught up in a severe knot. It accentuated her
fine profile and alluring neck line. Catching sight of old Link,
she waved a greeting, her smile warm and appealing.

Link said good-morning to Dennis Rafferty, the engineer,
and Pop Burke, the conductor. Young Junie Hanrahan, the
fireman, stuck his head out of the cab and jerked a nod. An
empty baggage truck stood on the depot platform. Link stopped
beside it. Glancing at his watch, he said, "We got 'bout half
an hour to wait. If they show up, we'll let 'em git aboard
the train before we make our move; I'll go in the front door;
you boys come up from behind. That sound okay?"

"That'll be all right," Rip answered. "Just be sure we have

them covered before you close in. We'll try to get away with it without any gun-play."

To the south, the Thunder River Range, which formed the southern and eastern barrier that shut Painted Meadows off from the rest of Colorado, looked as inhospitable as the San Cristobals, to the west. Link Easter caught Rip's contemplation of the mountains and read his thought.

"They can't git out of the Meadows by goin' over the mountains," he said. "They can try Mears Pass, but there'll be snow enough up there to turn them back for another week or two. If they know as much about this country as you boys figger they do, they took the snow into consideration. It means they just about got to go by train to git out of the Meadows. In a pinch, they might turn around and head back into Wyomin'."

Grumpy shook his head. "Not after the trouble they had at Bagleys. Where does this train stop after it leaves Lively? Chipeta?"

"No, Chipeta's just a ghost camp. A couple old-timers still putterin' around the mountain, but Chipeta ain't been a regular stop for over a year. On signal, Dennis Rafferty will stop anywheres, of course. But I thought of that and warned him and Pop to be careful who they picked up. If Morgan and his pardner try to flag a train, the crew will spot 'em and leave 'em standin' there." Old Link chuckled. "Pop and the boys are on their toes; that's why young Junie gave you a good lookin' over."

A young man drove up in a light wagon. Shouldering a mail sack, he carried it across the platform and stowed it away in the combination mail, express, baggage and passenger coach. The sheriff spoke to him.

"No express this mornin', Bob?"

"Not a thing, Link."

It was not the only indication that the Thunder River and Northern had fallen on lean days. Though the morning train was the only one out in twenty-four hours, not more than five or six passengers had taken seats in the coach. The little six-wheeler, the last locomotive belonging to the road, stood panting, anxious to be off, its brass work as brightly polished as ever. The steam box was leaking, however, and rust was showing through the paint on both engine and tender. Inside the coach, the red plush and ormolu that had once been the T.R. and N.'s pride, looked shabby and befouled.

Not counting a three-mile spur that ran up into the lower reaches of the San Cristobals, where railroad ties were still being cut and dressed, the Thunder River and Northern's operations had been confined to the scant forty-one miles of mainline from Lively down to White River Junction, where the standard gauge Denver and Pacific and the Colorado Midland had waged unending war on each other for years. But those forty-one miles were mountain miles, with hairpin curves and five-percent grades! The three-and-a-half-mile stretch through Ute Canyon, a deep, narrow gorge through the Thunder River Range, down which wild, mountain-fed Thunder River roared in tumultuous fury, was the worst of it, washing out track whenever it was in flood and leaving it a twisted mass of iron and dangling ties. Snowslides in winter often disrupted service for weeks on end! Railroading? It was madness! But Ute Canyon was the only natural cleft in all that granite barrier.

Rainbow strolled up the platform and back, glancing under the cars and making sure no one was riding the rods.

"Reckon you had yore trouble for nothin'," old Link remarked.

"I'm not overlooking any bets," Rip answered lightly. "We haven't long to wait now. Jim Wheelock told us the railroad is in bankruptcy. When did that happen?"

"Months ago. The court appointed Marcus Curry receiver. He's our local banker. The road's goin' to be put up at auction for its debts. It won't bring nothin'; nobody wants it." Link was only killing time with his chatter; his shrewd old eyes were alert and watchful. "It's goin' to be tough on Lively and the cowmen in the Meadows. The rails will be torn up for junk, I suppose, and we'll go back to havin' a toll-road down through Ute Canyon. That's what it was at first; when Dave Magoffin built it, he had no idea he was buildin' a railroad. At that time, the smoke of a locomotive had never been seen west of Denver."

"Dave Magoffin," the tall man repeated. "I remember him. The Thunder River and Northern was going strong when we were here last." He was only pretending to be interested in the affairs of the T.R. and N.; actually, his attention was focused on the street that ended at the depot, for that street, beyond Lively, was the main thoroughfare through Painted Meadows. From that direction, he believed, Morgan and Tovey would come, if they came at all.

"She was," Link agreed. "When Dave passed away, I reckon he figgered he was leaving Jeannie well provided for."

"Jeannie—the girl in the office?"

"Yeh, she's Dave's daughter. Girls don't come any nicer. She's tried to hold things together and keep the road goin'. She'd be better off without it, but it's a matter of pride with her. It's that way with Con Hanrahan, her superintendent, his son Junie and the others; they're workin' for little or nothin'. I reckon there was weeks before Mark stepped in when they didn't git paid at all."

"Wal, the Thunder River and Northern has outlived most of the narrow gauge roads that used to go tootin' off around the mountains in this State," Grumpy observed philosophically. The minutes were ticking away. If the bandits were to come, they had to come quickly now. "The Rio Grande Southern is still goin' strong," he rattled on. "Last I heard, the Argentine Central was still chuggin' up to the Georgetown district. They're about all that's—" he broke off abruptly and jerked out in quite another tone, "Look out! Watch that pile of lumber beyond the tracks! I got a flash of someone over there!"

The train was ready to leave. Jeannie stepped out of the depot and handed a sheet of yellow tissue to Pop Hughes, the conductor. The next moment Pop was bawlin, "All aboa-r-rd!" quite as though he believed there might be some last minute passengers. There weren't. Young Junie, who liked to steam out of Lively with a flourish, was using the whistle. With a weakish grunt, the drivewheels began to revolve.

"They didn't show up," old Link muttered, not trying to hide his disappointment.

Rip nodded soberly. "We've got our work cut out for us now. I—there they are!"

The train was moving faster. Two men had dashed out from behind the pile of lumber. Junie still had his hand on the whistle cord when Morgan grabbed the handrail and swung up into the cab. Old Dennis Rafferty's head was stuck out of the window on the other side. Before the engine crew knew what was happening, Morgan had them covered.

Mike Tovey climbed in after him.

Grumpy leaped for the coach and caught the rail at the rear steps. The best Rip could do was to grab a rung on the empty freight car. As soon as his feet found the iron step below, he managed to swing over the platform. Old Link, for all spryness, was left behind.

"We'll have to climb over the tender, Grump. You better let me handle this!"

"I'll be right there with you!" the little one answered. "Let's git up there before they cut the engine off!"

They ran through the swaying coach as the train sped on, faster and faster. The tender was piled high with cord wood. They reached it and flattened out there without attracting the bandits' attention. Morgan had the engineer covered; Tovey kept his gun on the fireman.

The partners exchanged a glance and inched forward a foot or two. That movement dislodged a stick of firewood. Morgan half turned, saw them and fired instantly, the slug ploughing a furrow up Rainbow's left arm.

Morgan no sooner shot than he dropped to his knees, where he was out of range. From that position, he raised his gun arm and began shooting blindly. His arm came up once too often. Timing it perfectly, Grumpy shot the gun out of the bandit's hand.

Tovey had dropped to his knees, too. Armed with Morgan's gun as well as his own, he crouched there, holding his fire until a face showed. When Rip pushed a piece of cordwood over the edge, it struck Tovey a glancing blow. Immediately he set his guns to bucking. Junie Hanrahan put a stop to that. Seizing a shovel, he brought it down on Tovey's head with a sickening thud that laid him out cold.

Old Dennis Rafferty, undaunted by all the shooting, grabbed the throttle and slapped on the brakes. As the train slowed, Morgan leaped out of the cab and landed sprawling on the right-of-way. Before he could get to his feet, Rip was on top of him. A sharp rap on the head with the barrel of his gun took all the fight out of Morgan.

Pop Burke came running as soon as the train stopped. He was excited, puffing. "I heard all that shooting up ahead and I didn't know what was happening. You fellas got both of them! What do you want me to do?"

"I want you to back up to the depot. My arm needs attention and so does Morgan's hand. See if you can get him to his feet."

Morgan got up groggily and was marched back to the train.

Leaning out of the cab, Grumpy got the tall man's attention. "Everythin's okay up here! We back up to the depot?"

"Yep!" Rip answered. "Stay where you are!"

He herded Morgan into the coach; the conductor went up to the engine. Presently, the train was backing toward Lively. The handful of passengers, chattering among themselves, stood up to get a better look at the bandit as Rainbow shoved him into a seat. Morgan cursed them and snarled at Rip. He had a long memory and had immediately recognized the tall man.

"Where in hell did you come from?" he jerked out viciously. "Can't a man pull a trick in this country without you and that little squirt showin' up?"

"Take it easy," Rainbow advised. "This is the last time we'll have to go after you. You left a dead man behind you in Salt Creek."

"So what?" Morgan flung back defiantly. His eyes were murderous as they focused on Rainbow's blood-soaked sleeve. "Too damn bad I didn't put that slug between your eyes!"

Rip smiled thinly. "You shouldn't have been so careless," he said lightly.

CHAPTER 6

THOUGH NEWS of the capture of the bandits spread quickly, only a small part of Lively's population turned out in time to see Morgan and Tovey, handcuffed together, marched up the main street to the jail.

When he had the two men safely locked up, Link led the way back to his office.

"I'm sorry I wasn't any help to you boys," he declared apologetically. "Like as not I'd have broke my neck if I'd tried to grab that train."

"I'm glad you didn't try," Rainbow told him. "As for not helping us, don't kid yourself, Link. Morgan told me he was in town last evening. It was their plan to flag the train between here and Chipeta, but when he heard that you had warned the crew not to pick up any strangers, he knew their scheme wouldn't work. So they tried it this way. We wouldn't have them locked up if it wasn't for you."

"That's right," Grumpy spoke up. "Our arrangement won't let us take the reward money, but there's no reason why you shouldn't git it."

The prisoners had been searched. All but a few dollars of the sum they had taken in Salt Creek was found on their persons.

"I'll stop at the bank and put this money where it'll be safe and then walk you over to Doc Trombly's office and let him dress yore arm," said Link. "You can sit here, Grumpy, and hold the fort. If Morgan starts squawkin' about his hand, tell him I'll have the doctor look at it directly."

They were gone an hour. When they returned, Rainbow carried his injured arm in a sling.

"Wal!" Grumpy exclaimed. "First time I ever saw you in that shape. Yore luck ran out on you at last."

"I figure it held pretty good," Rip returned, grinning. "I'll have to carry the arm this way for two or three days. In a week or so, the doctor says, it'll be as good as ever. He dug out the slug and took a few stitches." He turned to Link. "Are you going to stick around?"

"Till Doc gits through with Morgan," the old man answered. "I'll see that I have somebody here all the time. When I need a deputy, I can always swear in Charlie Hughes. How long do you figger it'll take the extradition papers to come through on those birds?"

"A week—ten days, unless they try to fight it. I don't believe they will. We'll get a wire off to Cheyenne and ask for an answer. Our job's finished. I expect we'll be heading for home tomorrow or the next day. Can you get these broncs back to Mal Bullard? No hurry about it, Link."

"Yeh, I'll take care of that," the sheriff promised. "Someone will be goin' up that way sooner or later. Bullard won't be in no shape to come for Morgan and Tovey. Who do you suppose they'll send down for 'em?"

"Let the Wyomin' authorities worry about it," said Grumpy. "They'll send someone down by way of Denver. To git out of here by train, we'll have to go around by Denver, too. We'll be all over Colorado gittin' there. By grab, that always floors me! Link, how far is it on a beeline to Denver?"

"'Bout eight-eighty-five miles, I'd say."

"And we'll have to travel three hundred and fifty to git

there! Someday, some smart gent will blast some tunnels through these mountains and a man will be able to git where he's goin' in a hurry . . . Come on, Rip; let's go down to the depot and git our wires off."

When they stepped up to the ticket window, they found Jeannie Magoffin alone in the office. They introduced themselves, which by now was unnecessary.

"We haven't had so much excitement in Lively since the big strike was made on Moran Mountain," Jeannie told them. "Won't you come in?" She unbolted the door. "You'll find telegraph blanks on the desk."

"You yore own operator?" the little man inquired.

Jeannie's green eyes twinkled. "The Thunder River and Northern is a one-woman proposition. I do about everything. So far, I haven't found it necessary to replace a broken rail."

"I'm sorry your train was delayed," said Rip, thinking how attractive she was. It wasn't merely that she was pretty; she had an intelligent face and there was a wholesomeness about her that was as refreshing as a touch of spring.

"It doesn't matter, Mr. Ripley," she said. "The passengers would have to lay over in White River Junction for two or three hours anyway. We do our best, but no one expects the T.R. and N. to be on time any more. You can't keep a railroad operating on spunk alone."

She said it lightly, but Rip saw her mouth tighten as she turned away. It made him realize that even the obvious admission that the decrepit little road was tottering to oblivion, did not come easy. Picking up a pencil, he wrote a telegram to Ferris Greenwood, in Cheyenne, and another to Mal Bullard, at Salt Creek.

Grumpy sat down across a desk from Jeannie. His likes and dislikes were always quickly taken and seldom changed. In his hard-bitten way, he was not easy to please, but something about Jeannie Magoffin had won him over completely.

"I don't want to pry into yore business, Miss Jeannie," he declared, "but Link's been tellin' us of the fight yo're puttin' up to keep the railroad goin'. I've seen the notices he's got tacked up around town, sayin' he's goin' to sell you out at auction on the courthouse steps, ten o'clock next Friday. You goin' to be able to do anythin' about it?"

"I'm afraid not. I've tried everything. Cut expenses to the bone. I'm cutting ties and shipping about two carloads a week. For a time, I was able to break even. But ties are down three dollars a hundred and the road's losing money every day."

"How many stockmen you got in the Meadows?" the little man asked.

"Quite a number. Twenty, at least."

Grumpy looked perplexed. "I don't git it; it's goin' to cost them money if they have to send their beef all the way to White River Junction on the hoof. They need your road. Do you mean to tell me they won't chip in to keep you goin'?"

"I've spoken to a number of them," Jeannie told him. "They've been advised not to put any money into the T.R. and N."

"Advised? Who advised 'em?"

"Mr. Curry, the receiver."

"Is that so?" The little man was really interested now. "He's the banker, eh?"

Jeannie nodded and said yes.

"Wal, I've known some bankers in my time. Most of 'em have ice water in their veins, but I always found their heads was in purty good condition. Didn't Link tell me Curry's got a ranch as well as the bank?"

"One of the best, Mr. Gibbs. C Bar."

Grumpy scratched his head thoughtfully. "There's an angle to this somewheres," he declared, his eyes puckered into a squint that was characteristic of him when he was cogitating. "If you'll pardon the question, Miss Jeannie—what's Curry's game? Has he got anythin' ag'in you personally?"

The question was unexpected. Jeannie caught her breath and some of the color ran out of her cheeks. "I—I'd rather not say," she murmured, unable to dissemble her embarrassment.

The little man was immediately apologetic. "I'm sorry. I didn't have no right to put my nose into yore affairs. I jest wanted to help you. I wish I could." Trying to save the situation with a laugh, he added, "I'm gittin' old, I reckon, talkin' out of turn. First thing I know, I'll be leanin' over the back fence, gabbin' like somebody's gran'ma. I wish we was goin' to be here for the auction. I'd like to see how it goes. You about finished, Rip?"

Rainbow had been finished for some time and was just listening to the conversation. He paid Jeannie for the telegrams. "We'll drop down later in the day and see if an answer has come."

"Of course, you'll be stopping at the Meadows," she said. "It's the best place in town."

"We haven't spoken for rooms yet," the tall man told her, "but I don't suppose they're crowded."

"No," she said laughingly, "I imagine you can have an entire floor if you ask for it."

The partners had no sooner left the depot than Rip took the little one to task. "What's got into you?" he scolded. "You usually have better sense than that. If this man Curry has something against the girl, you could find out from Link; you didn't have to ask her."

"By grab, I aim to ask him!" Grumpy declared with un-expected vehemence. "There's somethin' in this that don't meet the eye!"

Rainbow smiled. "Jeannie Magoffin made quite an impression on you."

"She's a fine girl, Rip. She's the sort that makes you feel glad to be a human bein'. I don't go around moanin' over other folks' troubles; I got my own. But when I see a fine young woman like her gittin' a raw deal, I git my dander up. In her place, most people would have tossed in the sponge long ago. The road can't be losin' much money; the town and the stockmen need it. Yo're always quick on the trigger. What's the deal? What's this man Curry's game?"

"I wouldn't know," Rainbow answered, with a minimum of interest. "Perhaps he feels the road is bound to get deeper and deeper into the red, and the best thing to do is to junk it now. He may be right. There's nothing we can do about it; we'll be on our way back to Black Forks tomorrow or the next day . . . Here's the hotel. We better see about registering."

That was quickly done. Their horses still stood at the hitchrack in front of the hotel. They mounted and rode down to Link Easter's office. The doctor had attended to Morgan and was leaving. The old man showed them the way back to his barn. On returning to the office, they made him a present of the camp outfit they had acquired in Bagleys.

"What about yore gear?" the latter inquired. "Yore saddles will be safe in the barn, but you can fetch 'em in here if you want."

"We hung them up," Grumpy told him. "We can leave 'em there for now. We'll sack 'em and pack our rifles when we know jest when we're leavin'." He pulled up a chair and got out his pipe. Knowing what was coming, Rip shook his head and sat down outside, in the sunshine. Through the open door, he heard the little one questioning Link about Marcus Curry.

"The stand Mark's takin' don't make sense to a lot of people," Link explained. "But it ain't no mystery to me. I know it's all on account of his boy, young Benton. Bent's sweet on Jeannie, and I reckon she feels the same way about him. You'd think the old goat would be tickled to death about it. But he ain't."

"You think that's the explanation?" Grumpy's tone was frankly dubious.

"I know it is! Mark's goin' to break up that affair if he possibly can. I reckon he figgers if the road closes up, Jeannie will have to go to Denver or somewheres and git a job and that'll end it."

The little one fell silent. And then: "Is Marcus Curry a half-wit?"

"I'll say he ain't!" Link declared stoutly. "He's a shrewd, hard-headed man. He had to be to git ahead the way he has."

"That's what I thought," Grumpy shot back. "If his son's in love with Jeannie Magoffin, Curry ain't idiot enough to believe that separatin' 'em will break it up. He's got another iron in the fire, Link. He's jest throwin' dust in folks' eyes by purtendin' to make a big cry and holler about not lettin' his boy marry that girl."

"I don't believe it!" Rainbow heard the old man bring his chair down on all fours with an angry bang. "Mark's an honorable man! He don't want the T.R. and N. What could he do with it?"

"I don't know," Grumpy muttered. "I can't figger it out. I wish I could. It keeps puzzlin' me and I can't git it outa my mind. I'd like to have a talk with young Curry."

"You'll perhaps have the chance," Link said crustily. "He comes into town most every afternoon."

"He don't work in the bank?"

Anything further he might have said would have been drowned out by a commotion that began suddenly beyond the partition that divided the office from the cell tier, in the rear.

"What the hell is that?" the old man cried. "Sounds like they're tearin' the jail down!"

Rainbow got out of his chair and stepped inside as Link flung open the connecting door. Morgan and Tovey were banging heavy wooden stools against the doors of their cells.

"Stop that racket!" Link yelped. "What's the idea?"

"We ain't eat since yesterday noon!" Morgan growled. "We want some grub!"

"You do, eh? Will fried chicken and strawberry shortcake suit you?"

Link wasn't in the habit of baiting his prisoners, but he was mad now. Bristling, he walked back to the cells.

"Don't give us none of your lip, you old butterball!" Morgan jerked out fiercely. "I tell you, we want somethin' to eat!"

"You'll git somethin' at twelve o'clock—and if you do any more bangin' with them stools, bread and water is what you'll git!"

That seemed to end it. Link was still out in back when a stockily-built man walked into the office. His hair was gray and so was his carefully-tended mustache. He was not only better dressed then the run of Lively's citizens but there was an unmistakable air of prosperity and authority about him. The partners gathered at once that he was Marcus Curry. Any doubt of it was dispelled a moment later.

"Hi, Mark," Link greeted him. "I'm glad you dropped in; I want you to meet these gentlemen." After introducing the partners, he said, "That pair I got locked up have stuck up their last bank, I reckon."

"I hope so," Curry replied. "I wanted to ask you, Ripley, if you have warrants for them."

"No, whoever comes down for them will bring the warrants along with the extradition papers," the tall man replied. "I suppose you have a reason for asking."

The banker nodded. "I was just thinking that without warrants, Link can't hold them indefinitely unless he brings some charges against them."

"I can hold 'em two or three days on suspicion," the sheriff informed him.

"That won't be long enough. The Governor will have to sign the papers. According to the Denver *Post* he's off somewhere dedicating a monument."

"Wal, I can charge 'em with holdin' up a train and assault with a deadly weapon, if I have to," old Link grumbled. He didn't relish being told what to do.

"You do it today or tomorrow," Curry informed him bluntly. "I don't want it to run over into Friday; you got the auction to take care of."

"Hell, that won't take but a few minutes," Link protested.

"I hope not," Curry snapped. "I want you to be sure it goes off on time."

He had been gone a minute or two, when Grumpy observed with withering sarcasm, "You got him sized up right, Link; Marcus Curry is certainly an honorable man. He don't want Jeannie's railroad—not much!" He glared at the sheriff and Rainbow with a fine show of indignation. "One of you tells me all old money-bags is doin' is closin' up the road before it gits deeper in the red; the other one says all he's got on his mind is keepin' his boy from marryin' the girl . . . Wal, is a loud silence the only answer I can git out of you?"

Link sat down heavily. "By gum, I don't know what to think. He's the receiver; he knows I can't accept a bid from him."

"Huh!" the little one snorted. "He'll be smarter than that; he'll have a dummy bid it in for him, and he'll walk off with it for less than it's worth as scrap iron!" He flicked off a glance at Rip. "I suppose yo're goin' to tell me ag'in that it's none of my business."

The tall man pulled down the corners of his mouth and gave him a sober and thoughtful answer. "It's none of your business, Grump; and it's none of mine. But that needn't stop us from making it our business."

Link swung around in his chair. "What do you mean by that?" he demanded sharply, sensing the threat in Rainbow's remark.

"I mean that Grump is right," was the latter's soft answer; "friend Curry is dealing with a stacked deck. I was anxious to be on my way home, but I won't mind a bit now if we're stuck here a few days."

Link Easter's eyes narrowed. "You better go slow," he advised. "I'm all for Jeannie Magoffin. I know Mark ain't givin' her a break; I wouldn't expect him to; he's never given anybody a break. But that doesn't make him a crook. Yo're jumpin' to conclusions, Rainbow."

"I'm not jumping to anything," Rip contradicted, with a thin smile. "I'm just becoming a little curious, Link."

CHAPTER 7

ON RETURNING to the depot early in the afternoon, Jeannie handed them a telegram. It was a brief congratulatory message from Ferris Greenwood, filed at Cheyenne. It was followed, half an hour later, by a much longer message from him asking the partners to remain in Lively until the extradition papers came through. He said that he had been in touch by wire with Bullard, at Salt Creek; Mal was sending a deputy to Cheyenne, where he was to be joined by a detective supplied by the Cheyenne police department.

Rainbow handed the message to the little one.

"It's no disappointment to me," Grumpy declared, when he read it. "'No delay at this end,' he says. 'Will leave for Denver this evening to expedite matters there.' That seems to be the story. I'm surprised he doesn't tell us not to leave Morgan and Tovey out of our sight. That's why he's holdin' us here; figgers they might bust away from Link."

They did not attempt to sound Jeannie out any further on the sale of the road. This was at Rainbow's insistence; he felt that if the information they wanted was to be secured at all, it was not likely to be had from her.

She was aware of their friendly interest. It prompted her to say, "The northbound is due in at 5:20. I always stay on till six. I'll keep the key open for you; you'll perhaps have something further coming through. I could stay on later, if you think it's necessary."

"No need to do that," Rip told her. "We'll drop back a little after five. If there's anything later, it can come through in the morning."

They spent the afternoon wandering about town, listening to the talk on the street and in the saloons. They were known by sight and had no difficulty in getting into conversation whenever they pleased.

"What do you make of it, Rip?" the little man queried, after they had sampled public opinion in a dozen places. "Some of these folks are scared, but there don't seem to be any idea of gittin' together and puttin' it up to Curry to call off the sale."

"I think they've had this thing hanging over their heads so long they've got used to it," said Rainbow. "They've seen the Thunder River and Northern going from bad to worse for several years. Something has always kept it rolling. Half the people we've talked to seem to feel that it isn't going to fold even now."

They had passed Louie Bannerman's general store several times. He was Lively's leading merchant. Rip suggested that they drop in there and see what he had to say.

They were making a trifling purchase of a clerk, when a squat, balding little man came up to them and introduced himself as the proprietor. After some preliminary talk about the capture of bandits, Grump said guilelessly, "What are you folks goin' to do when you lose the railroad? Lively will dry up and blow away, won't it?"

Louie shrugged and smiled enigmatically. "If I have to pull up stakes, I can do it. I ain't gonna start packing just yet."

"I suppose that's the way to feel," said Rip. "But wouldn't

it be a good idea for you merchants and the cowmen in the valley to get together and try to persuade Curry to call off his wolf."

"I tried it." Louie shook his head. "They're afraid of him; a little note at his bank, or a mortgage. You know how that goes. I don't owe him a cent; I can say what I please. He don't scare me. I've know him for twenty years and I never caught him biting off his nose to spite his face."

"There's always a first time," Grumpy observed.

"No, not that kind of a first; there's nothing Mark Curry loves half so much as a dollar. Where's the business going to come from for his bank if Lively dries up? He's got cattle to ship. He gets along with a small crew. He'll need a big crew if he has to trail his beef all the way to White River Junction... No, he's got a trick up his sleeve. The T.R. and N. is only losing a couple thousand a year; debts of about twelve to fifteen thousand. Any little mining excitement will put it back in the black."

"Trouble down in Ute Canyon could change the picture in a hurry," Rip reminded him. "Snowslide—flood—"

"I know." Louie nodded in confirmation of his opinion. "Miss Jeannie is being forced out; that's all there is to this."

Back on the street, the partners were of two minds about what they had just heard.

"He's got it sized up about right," Grumpy declared. "He said only what I been sayin'. You think there's more to it, eh?"

"I think Curry is playing for bigger stakes than taking over a defunct narrow railroad. I wish I could put my finger on it. I'm for the underdog every time—especially when it happens to be someone as young and lovely as this Magoffin girl. But our sympathy isn't going to help her any, Grump. There isn't a thing we can do for her unless we know what the game is."

They were at the depot again shortly after five. A brief message had arrived from Bullard, confirming Greenwood's statement that a deputy had left Salt Creek for Cheyenne.

"He don't sound too friendly," Grumpy remarked. "Reckon

Mal's beatin' his gums because he wasn't in on capturin' 'em. He could have been if he hadn't made such a fool play."

He and Rip decided to wait for the train. The empty baggage truck still stood on the station platform. They seated themselves on it and had been there only a few minutes when a handcar was seen moving toward them from the south. A tall, rawboned man, lean as a rail, was pumping it. When he reached the depot, he pulled the car off the track and hurried inside.

"Irish as Paddy's pig," Grumpy said. "Who do you figger he might be?"

"If Link described him correctly, he might be Con Hanrahan, the superintendent of this vest pocket railroad."

It was a shrewd surmise. Con had just come down from the camp where Jeannie had a gang cutting and loading ties. His title of superintendent was simply a carry-over from better days; actually, he was the handyman and Jack-of-all-trades for the T.R. and N. Had she asked him to carry the road over the mountains on his back, he would have done his best to oblige. He was that kind.

He wasn't inside more than a few minutes. When he stepped out, he approached the partners, his step long and brisk. "I'm Hanrahan," he said, as though that were identification enough. "Miss Jeannie says you're the boys that captured them t'ieves this morning. She also says the lad did his bit, too." Seeing that they didn't understand his reference to his son, he added, "Young Connie, I mean; they call him Junie, short for Junior."

"He shore did more'n his bit," Grumpy told him. "You shoulda seen him use his shovel on Tovey's skull. It laid him out. I'm glad he didn't spit on his hands first; I'm afraid he'd have killed him."

Praise of his son was the way to Con Hanrahan's heart. "He's a fine boy. A better man than I was at twenty-two— and in more ways than one."

"How do you mean that?" Rip asked.

"Well, it's this way," Con's blue eyes twinkled merrily. "Junie only fights for his principles; when I was a young buck, I fought just for the fun of it."

They laughed together and were quickly acquainted.

"Sit down here with us a minute, Con," Rip invited. "I'd like to ask you a question or two that we can't put to Miss Magoffin . . . Con—who's after this road? The Midland or the Denver and Pacific?"

"Naw, they don't want it. When she saw how t'ings were going, she tried to unload it on them. Neither one of 'em was interested at any price. They can't see any business for the road. It wouldn't do any good to run it up through the Meadows and over into the coal field in Wyoming; the Laramie and North Park is almost there now. They'd git there first and sew t'ings up."

"If it isn't that—then what is the game?" Rip persisted.

"Shure and I don't know! I wisht I could tell you." Con pulled out a red bandanna and blew his nose violently. "It's a crooked scheme of some sort, of that I'm certain." A belated sense of caution made him regard the partners carefully for a moment. "Do you mind saying what interest you have in it?"

"Not at all," Grumpy informed him. "Miss Jeannie is gittin' a raw deal. We're held up here for a few days. We'd like to help her if we could."

"I t'ank you for that," Con said. "If you've been inquiring, you've heard the talk around town about the little lady and Bent Curry. Pay no attention to it. I t'ink Mark started it himself. The likes of him objecting to his son paying court to Miss Jeannie! The idea of it! The devil himself couldn't turn Bent ag'in her, nor her ag'in him."

"Have any strangers been here lately, visitin' Curry?" Grumpy asked.

"Not that I know of. But he's been running to Denver ofterner than usual."

The little one was not impressed. "His business could account for that."

"Not if it didn't account for it in the past," Rip argued. "This might be a lead—the first one we've picked up. Tell me, Con—has Curry ever been interested in any mining ventures?"

"Shure! I'd say he's put in more'n he's taken out."

"But he might be interested, eh?"

"Could be. But mining's dead in Painted Meadows. There's a couple lads roaming over Moran Mountain. But they ain't looking for gold."

"What are they looking for?" Rainbow asked.

"Uranium, they say."

"That could be better than gold. It would mean ore that would have to be shipped out."

"Wal!" Grumpy exclaimed. "I was wonderin' what you was drivin' at. I'm beginnin' to git yore drift... You mean that Curry may be in on a sleeper and is holdin' back till he gits the road?"

"I don't mean anything; I'm just grabbing at straws," the tall man confessed. "Are those men the ordinary run of prospectors, Con?"

"No, they use words a yard long—not that they have much to say. But they know what they're doing, shure enough."

"All right," said Rip. "We've got horses; we'll ride down there tomorrow and have a look around."

From far away to the south came the melancholy blast of a train whistle.

"That's Number 2, rolling through Chipeta," Con announced. He glanced at his huge watch. "She's right on the dot, for a change."

A handful of townspeople had come down to meet the train. The partners dismissed them with a glance and focused their attention on the young horseman who rode up to the depot and flung himself from the saddle. Hastily tethering his bronc, he swung around the corner of the shabby little building and darted inside. There was the bronzed look of a rangeman about him, a six-footer and narrow hipped. He was tight of lip and pre-occupied.

"Bent Curry," Con muttered. "He's got something on his mind; he don't usually move that fast. Had a row with his old man, no doubt—I don't like to disturb you, boys, but I better run the truck up the platform; there should be some express this evening. I'll see you later."

"So that's young Curry," Grumpy remarked, as he and Rip slipped down. "You said somethin' about wantin' to have a talk with him."

Rainbow shook his head. "I've changed my mind, for the present; I don't believe he could tell us a thing we haven't heard."

Link Easter arrived as the train steamed in. "Charlie is on duty at the jail," he explained. "I always like to see who's hittin' town."

A brief flurry of excitement followed. Link identified the passengers as local people. "The woman with the flock of kids is Lem Spade's wife—you passed his ranch on yore way down the Meadows—the rest live right here in town."

The partners walked back to the jail with Link and talked with Charlie Hughes, his deputy, for a few minutes.

"Whatever you do," Grumpy cautioned him, "don't go near them cells tonight with the keys on you, or a gun. Those birds are cute; give 'em a chance and they'll fox up on you. We don't want to lose 'em, Charlie."

"They won't put anythin' over on me," the latter assured him.

"I'll drop in this evening and see how things are going," Rainbow said, as he and Grumpy were leaving.

Link accompanied them as far as the hotel. "Young Bent was in town this afternoon."

"We saw him," Grumpy replied.

"Have anythin' to say to him?"

"No, Rip thought it wouldn't git us anywhere."

"Like as not it wouldn't," the old man agreed. "He and Mark had one hell of an argument at the bank. You could hear Mark yellin' clear acrost the street. A showdown was bound to come."

Rip offered no comment, but Grumpy said, "I hope it sheds some light on this business. It'll have to come quick to do any good."

Link left them and they went up to their rooms to refresh themselves before supper. Grumpy was muttering.

"What's your trouble?" Rip demanded.

"It's like bangin' yore head ag'in a stone wall," the little one grumbled. "We've cracked some big cases, but this thing's got me buffaloed."

"Suppose we forget it for tonight." Rip's tone had a sharp edge of annoyance. "We'll see what we can do about it tomorrow. After all, we're being paid mighty well for sticking here in Lively. Let's give that a little thought."

Grumpy looked up, puzzled and ready to take exception to anything he didn't like. "What's the meanin' of that crack?"

"I want you to turn in early and leave a call for one o'clock. After supper, I'll go back to the jail and stay there until you show up. You can stick it out, then, till daylight."

The little one stared at him incredulously. "Good grief!" he exploded. "Yo're lookin' for trouble where they ain't none! Morgan and Tovey are a couple of lone wolves; they got no one on the outside who might try to get into 'em!"

"I know it," Rainbow acknowledged. "I don't expect any trouble. During the day, with Link on the job, I feel safe enough. But when something goes wrong, it always happens at night. I'd rather sit up than lay awake worrying about it."

CHAPTER 8

THE NIGHT passed uneventfully. When the partners sat down to a late breakfast, Grumpy was in a crusty temper.

"I hope yo're satisfied," he grumbled. "That pail's an old one, but it'll hold that pair as long as there's any need of keepin' 'em there."

"I'm satisfied that we got by last night without any trouble," said Rip. "We'll play it the same way this evening and every night as long as we've got Morgan and Tovey on our hands. If you want to grab some sleep, go ahead; we can ride down to Chipeta this afternoon."

"No, I had sleep enough," the doughty little man snapped. "Let's be on our way."

As soon as they mentioned Chipeta and Moran Mountain to Link, he divined their purpose. "You'll be wastin' yore time, boys. But go ahead!"

They found Chipeta no different from other ghost camps they had known; when the mines failed, the population had simply picked up and moved out. The fire that usually wipes out a deserted camp had not occurred as yet, but the flimsy shacks and tinder-dry stores and saloons were just waiting for the match.

They found the two young men who were prospecting for uranium and talked with them at length. They had taken possession of the most comfortable cabin in the camp and spent the winter on the mountain, and without success. Though the partners tried, they were unable to punch any holes in the prospectors' story, and they returned to Lively convinced that they had made the trip for nothing.

They received a surprise—in fact, several—when the evening train pulled in. The first man to step down was Ferris Greenwood. He was accompanied by the deputy from Salt Creek and the Cheyenne detective. Other arrivals included two reporters and a staff photographer, representing Denver newspapers, in Lively to cover the capture of the bandits. Not unnoticed by the partners were two others, men of affairs, by their appearance.

"We hadn't expected to see you," Rainbow said, as he shook hands with Greenwood.

"I made the trip for a couple reasons," the latter explained. "The Governor is away; it'll be several days before the papers can be signed. But we've got authority to remove the prisoners to the Denver city prison. And there is the matter of the reward. The company's always made it a point to take care of such things promptly. According to your telegram, Sheriff Easter is entitled to it."

"He is," Grumpy spoke up. "Link wasn't in on the actual capture, but if it hadn't been for his foresight, we might have missed 'em." If he was being generous, it was no less than he intended; he knew Link could use the thousand dollars.

The reporters were querying Link. The little one called him over and introduced him to Greenwood. It embarrassed the old man to hear himself praised.

"You better be careful," he protested, "or my head will be gittin' too big for my hat. I don't know whether the money should be comin' to me, by rights, but if you all say so, I'll be mighty pleased to git it. Them reporters was buzzin' me,

.I told 'em to talk to you. You boys want to take 'em on now or later? They'd like to catch the mornin' train back."

"Let's get it over with as quickly as possible," said Rip. He and the little one never sought publicity, feeling that in their calling there was some advantage in keeping their names and pictures out of newspapers. "Before you call them over, Link—did you recognize the two gentlemen who spoke to the conductor as they got off the train?"

"No, they're strangers. They may be showin' up for the sale tomorrow."

"That's what I was thinking." Rainbow turned to Greenwood and asked if he had become acquainted with the men, on the train.

"I saw them in the diner this morning and sat down with them later in the observation car; but I didn't become acquainted with them. Perhaps these newspapermen can tell you who they are, Rip."

Rainbow beckoned to the reporters and put his question to them. "They're two well-known Denverites," one informed him. "The man in the gray suit is Alvin Ketchel, the lawyer; the other is Miles Colton, the banker."

The partners exchanged an understanding glance. Whether Ketchel and Colton were there to bid in the Thunder River and Northern for Mark Curry, or for themselves, remained to be seen; but that the three were acting in collusion was beyond question in their minds.

The partners tried to make the interview as brief as possible but the story of the fight on the speeding train was such good copy that the newspapermen insisted on the details. When they turned to Link, the old man put them off.

"Take yore pictures now, but if you want to talk to me, you'll have to come to the office; I got a deputy on duty and it's time for him to go out to supper."

The reporters stepped into the depot to arrange with Jeannie about filing their stories that evening. The others walked up the street together.

"With two Wyoming peace officers on the job, I take it

that our responsibility in regard to Morgan and Tovey has ended," Rainbow said to Greenwood.

"Yes, and you've turned in another excellent job. This gentleman from Salt Creek will have to go into court in the morning and present his authority for removing the prisoners from this county. It will take only a few minutes but it means we won't be able to leave before Saturday's train. Will the two of you wait over and leave with us?"

"That'll suit me," Grumpy spoke up quickly. "I don't want to miss the doin's here tomorrow. The narrow gauge is goin' to be sold at auction, for debts. Be quite some excitement, I reckon. It's goin' to leave this section of Colorado without a railroad."

"Is that so?" Greenwood's thin features and tight little mouth expressed his surprise and concern. "I'm sorry to hear that; we have an account in Lively. We've had the coverage on the bank for some years. I'll have to see Mr. Curry."

It was enough to stop the partners from saying more.

They had supper with Greenwood. Ketchel, the Denver attorney, and his companion were seated across the dining room. They returned Greenwood's friendly nod. With supper out of the way, the partners had a minute or two alone.

"It might be wise to slip Link the word not to repeat anything we've had to say about this railroad deal," Rip advised. "We'll walk over to Link's office with Greenwood; you get the old man aside. We won't linger there long; if we have the right hunch on Ketchel and his friend, they'll get in touch with Curry this evening. We'll keep an eye on them."

"If they figger they're bein' watched," the little one countered, "they won't risk gittin' together."

"Why should they be suspicious?"

"I dunno. I'm still up a tree on this business. There ain't money enough involved in the deal for Curry to need any help from a Denver bank. And why bring in a high-priced lawyer?"

Rainbow was unable to give him a valid answer.

After spending a few minutes at the sheriff's office, they strolled up the street. Three men—cowpunchers by their look—were seated on the wooden steps in front of Louie Bannerman's store. The partners found a spot for themselves and settled down to watching the bank. A light burned within.

They had not been waiting long when Ketchel and Colton appeared. They rapped on the bank door. Curry admitted them at once.

"Wal, I reckon that's it!" Grumpy muttered. "No guess work about it now; they got a deal on the fire!"

Rainbow had nothing to say as they walked away. At the hotel, they ran into Jennings and Wheeler, the Denver newspapermen, who had just finished filing their stories and had a long evening on their hands.

"You fellows wouldn't like to play a little bridge, would you?" Jennings asked.

Grumpy left it to Rip to answer, expecting him to say no. To his surprise, the tall man said, "We'll be delighted. We're on the second floor. Get some cards and come up when you're ready."

"What was the idea of that?" Grumpy demanded, as the two of them ascended the stairs. "You don't want to play cards no more than I do."

"You're right about that," Rainbow admitted, with a smile. "It just occurred to me that it might be a good bet to cultivate those boys. I'd like to know something more about Alvin Ketchel and Mr. Miles Colton. They may be able to fill us in a bit."

The card game had proceeded for some minutes, when he said, "You boys may be running away from a story ten times as important as the capture of a couple bank bandits in pulling out on the morning train."

"You mean the sale of this junk heap known as the Thunder River and Northern?" Jennings inquired, with a chuckle.

Rip nodded. "It may mean more than you think."

"Around here, yes; but it won't make a ripple over the rest of the State."

"Would you still be of that opinion if I were to tell you that Ketchel and Colton are here to bid it in?"

The reporters put down their cards and regarded him keenly for a moment.

"How sure are you?" Wheeler asked.

"I'm sure. Ketchel is a big shot lawyer, isn't he?"

"He was head counsel for the Denver and Pacific for seven, eight years. He doesn't play for peanuts."

"What about Miles Colton?" the tall man queried. "Is he interested in railroads?"

"With his dough?" Jennings laughed sarcastically. "I suppose he owns stock in a dozen roads . . . What are they going to do with this little narrow gauge line?"

Rainbow shrugged. "I don't know. Maybe they're going to junk it. It's too late to get a wire off tonight, but why don't you stick around and put that question up to your editors, first thing in the morning?"

"I'm damned if I don't," said Jennings. He turned to Wheeler. "What do you think about it, Bill?"

"If Ripley's right, there's a rat in the woodpile. I don't believe Colton would be calling in an expensive gent like Alvin Ketchel if he was going to junk this one-horse road." He flashed a glance at Rainbow. "Have you and your partner got a finger in the pie?"

"No, we're just interested bystanders. The road's been in trouble for a long time. Miss Magoffin has put up a great fight to keep it going. Mark Curry, the local banker, got himself appointed receiver. Now she's being squeezed out. We don't like the smell of it."

"Who would? But that's the way it goes, Rip. Anything to make a dollar, and to hell with who gets hurt . . . You say you're sure they're here to bid in the road. Off the record, can't you give us some idea of what you base that on?"

"I can—if you'll agree not to put it up to them until after the sale. If you questioned them now, all you'd get would be a frosty 'No comment.'"

"Go ahead," Wheeler urged. "You've got my word."

"And mine," Jennings seconded.

"They're·in the bank right now with Curry. That ought to

tell you enough. I don't imagine they're discussing the weather."

"It's enough for me," said Jennings.

"And me," Wheeler agreed. "I'll stay over." He picked up his cards. He had to study them a minute before he could focus his attention on them. "I'll bid four spades."

CHAPTER 9

AT GREENWOOD'S request, the partners accompanied him and the two officers to the courthouse at nine the next morning. Authorization for the transfer of Morgan and Tovey was presented to the judge. He read the papers and affixed his signature. That was all there was to it.

It had taken only a few minutes, and yet when Rip and Grumpy stepped out of the courthouse, they found a crowd beginning to gather for the auction.

"Don't see anythin' of our friends Jennings and Wheeler," the little man observed.

"It's early. They're waiting at the depot, no doubt. Let's go back to the hotel; the arrangement was that they'd look us up there as soon as they got any word from Denver."

It got to be nine-forty-five. By now there was a general movement toward the courthouse steps. The men who passed the hotel window, where Rip and Grumpy sat, looked stern and sober. They were not all townspeople; from the bits of conversation the partners overheard, they knew that Uncle Joe Corbett, Lem Spade, Dutch Altmeyer and half a dozen other cowmen from the valley had ridden in. Cowboys passed, their spur chains jangling pleasantly on the plank sidewalk. Their manner indicated that their interest in the proceedings was not limited to satisfying their curiosity; what became of the T.R. and N. could not help but affect their livelihood, and they seemed to realize it.

Colton and Ketchel came down the stairs together and left the hotel for the courthouse.

"We better be goin', too," Grumpy muttered. "It's ten of ten."

"Let's give the boys another minute or two," Rip suggested. "Here they come now."

"Nothing doing," Jennings told them. "We haven't had a word. Miss Magoffin wants to be at the sale. We couldn't ask her to wait any longer."

Jeannie passed the window a moment later. Young Bent Curry was with her.

"All right," said Rainbow. "We better get up there."

They pushed through the crowd and found Ferris Greenwood on the steps. Mark Curry stood a few feet away, a wooden expression on his round face. Colton and Ketchel had taken a position to Curry's right, but he pretended not to be aware of them.

It was a minute or two of ten when Link Easter stepped out of the courthouse. He drew his watch and held it in his hand, waiting until it was exactly ten o'clock.

"By order of the District Court and the authority invested in me," he began, reading from a legal document, "I offer for sale to the highest bidder, the right of way, rollin' stock, tools and any and all other equipment and buildings, together with bills payable, the Thunder River and Northern Railroad."

It was a grim business for the old man. A list of the "any and all other equipment" had been prepared for him. He went through it, item by item. Finished, he glared at the crowd, and particularly at Marcus Curry.

"What am I bid?" he rapped. "What do I hear?"

"Four thousand!" came from Miles Colton.

Link fastened his irate eyes on the man. "That'd be stealin' it . . . do I hear another bid?"

"Five thousand!" Ketchel called out.

Link had his two bids that the law required; the T.R. and N. would have to be sold now. He stalled, pleaded for more bidding but got none.

"All right!" he growled. "Six thousand I'm bid! If yo're through—six thousand once—six thousand twice—"

"Seventy-five hundred!" Grumpy piped up, to the amazement of Rainbow and the other bidders.

"Sold!" old Link bawled.

It was Grumpy's turn to be amazed. The crowd cheered, sensing that Curry's plans had miscarried. The latter was beside himself. "You doddering old fool, you don't know what you're doing!" he burst out, as he rushed at Link. "This auction's got to be conducted according to law!" He shook his fist at the old man. "You listen to me! You haven't sold this railroad! You reopen the bidding and give these other men a chance!"

Colton, no less infuriated, would have joined in the argument, but the cooler-headed Ketchel restrained him.

"Yore friends had their chance, Mark!" Link flung back angrily. "I ain't called on to wait here all day for 'em to make up their minds! The Thunder River and Northern is sold to Gibbs—and that's final!"

The crowd tittered at Curry's expense. Its amusement was cut short as Ketchel took a hand.

"Mr. Sheriff," he said, employing his best courtroom manner, "the terms of the sale require a deposit of twenty-five percent in cash, or by certified check, the balance payable within thirty days." He glanced at Grumpy. "Is Mr. Gibbs prepared to fulfill those terms?"

The little man opened up on him fiercely. "Are you tryin' to tell these folks my check ain't good for seventy-five hundred dollars?"

"I don't know what your check is worth," Ketchel returned. "The terms were plainly stated—certified check or cash. If you're not in a position to comply, it's no sale."

Mark Curry added his voice to the argument.

"Just a minute, Mr. Curry," Greenwood spoke up. "I've known Mr. Gibbs for years. I'll be happy to give you the cash for all or part of his bid, as he pleases."

Rainbow grabbed the little one's arm. Under his breath he said, "Here's your chance to get out of this. What could you do with a railroad? You don't want it, do you?"

"I didn't want it; I was jest tryin' to run up the figger for Jeannie. But, by grab, I want it now! That dude from Denver ain't showin' me up!"

The excitement was over and the crowd began to drift away. Jeannie reached the little man. There were tears in her eyes.

"What you cryin' about?" he queried gruffly. "You're still in business."

"But I've lost the road. What do you want me to do, Mr. Gibbs."

"I want you to go on jest as you been doin' till I git time to catch my breath. If Mark Curry tries to make you take any of his sass, you let me know; I'll take care of him."

Curry had left the steps, with Colton and Ketchel. With their going, Link slapped a hoary hand on Grumpy's shoulder.

"By gum, I sold you a railroad, Grumpy!" he cackled.

"You mean you stuck me with one!"

"Stuck you, nothin'! Them fellas will make you an offer to sell out at a profit the minute they git you in a corner! I ain't so slow; I saw what the game was. Mark wanted them to have it, and they was just goin' to pass the ball back and forth between 'em." He jerked his head in Greenwood's direction. "You git the cash and we'll close up this deal."

Greenwood nodded. "Let's walk down to the bank. You hand me your check, Grumpy, and I'll endorse it or get the cash. How much do you want to pay now?"

"All of it!" the little one growled. "My balance can stand it!"

Rainbow had nothing to say; he realized it was too late for words. And yet, when he found himself alone with Grumpy ten minutes later, he could hold in no longer. "You've done some crazy things in your life, but this tops everything! What do you propose to do—pull out of Lively tomorrow and leave Miss Magoffin to run your railroad?"

"I don't know what I'm gonna do," was the little man's flinty answer. "If I'm stuck, I'm stuck. You won't hear me squawkin' about it. As for runnin' the road, I don't know who could do a better job than Jeannie Magoffin. I couldn't do it, myself."

"I'm glad to hear you say that," Rip declared, in his exasperation. "You don't know what you've let yourself in for. Where'll you be if a flood rips out a mile of track in Ute Canyon or a snowslide puts you out of business for a month or two? You'll lose everything you've got. I know that girl was getting a raw deal; I'm a human being; I've got feelings, too. You're letting your feelings run away with your good sense."

"Suppose we let it go at that for the present," Grumpy complained, a harried look on his hard-bitten face. "We'd agreed that we needed a little vacation and wouldn't take a case for a few weeks, when we got that hurry-up call from Greenwood. If you're anxious to git back to Wyomin' go ahead; I'll stick around here a while."

The tall man shook his head. "I'm not leaving you behind so you can do something even more foolish. You need looking after, and you're going to get it."

To get away from the crowd in the hotel lobby, they went directly to their rooms. The morning was warm. Grumpy dragged a chair to an open window. It always helped his mental processes to pull of his boots. Slouched down in the chair, his grizzled face screwed up into a thoughtful knot, he puffed his pipe and refused to be drawn into conversation.

They had been upstairs but a few minutes, when someone rapped on the door. Rip opened it. Miles Colton stood there.

"I'd like to speak to your partner. May I come in?"

"Come right ahead," Rainbow told him.

Grumpy straightened up on recognizing his visitor.

"I'll get to the point in a hurry," Colton said, with the

brusqueness of one who is used to having his way. "Do you want to make a quick profit on your deal?"

The little man looked him over carefully. "What do you mean by a profit?"

"I'll give you ten thousand for the road."

Though he was sorely tempted to say yes, Grumpy shook his head. Bluffing now, he said, "I ain't interested. I got some plans for the Thunder River and Northern."

"I'll make it fifteen."

It met with a flat no. Unabashed, Colton said, "You've got your price. I won't haggle with you. I'll give you twenty-five thousand cash."

"Wal!" Grumpy exclaimed. "Looks like you're bein' smoked out. You really want the road, don't you?"

"I want it, and I mean to have it!"

Without a by-your-leave, Rainbow injected himself into the argument. "You'll never get it that way," he declared pointedly. "If the T.R. and N. is worth twenty-five thousand to you, it's worth twenty-five thousand to us."

"I've given you my best offer." Miles Colton's patience was wearing thin. "You can take it or leave it!"

"The road is not for sale—at the present time," Rip informed him.

"Is that final?"

"It is," Grumpy declared adamantly.

"Very well!" Infuriated now, Colton swung around and reached the door. From there, he said, "I'll bring you to terms! You're asking for trouble, and you'll get it!"

He slammed the door and left a charged silence behind him that endured until Grumpy had pulled on his boots.

"Wal?" the little one demanded irascibly of Rainbow. "You called me ten kinds of a fool for buyin' that junk pile. What you got to say now?"

"We've got hold of something, Grump. I'm ready to eat crow."

"Is that so? And what's the meanin' of that 'we' stuff?"

Rainbow grinned. "I want to buy some chips in this game.

I don't know what kind of trouble he expects to dish out to us, but I want fifty percent of that, too."

"Wal, by damn, you've got it! We'll see this thing through together!" Grumpy was too well pleased to make any attempt to conceal the fact. "You sit down and write Judge Carver that we'll be home when we git there, and not before. And you can do a little pen scratchin' for half of that seventy-five hundred." He shook his head in honest bewilderment. "I admit I didn't know what I was doin' when I put in that bid, but it seems I might have stuck my noggin right into a diamond tiara." He reached for his hat. "Suppose we look up them reporters. If they ain't downstairs, we'll try the depot."

"Better not mention anything about Colton's offer," Rainbow advised.

"It can wait," the little man agreed. "But there's one thing I want understood. We don't know what Colton's got up his sleeve. But it's way up in the blue chips, whatever it is. Before he throws any trouble at us, he'll likely come back with another offer. Mebbe as much as fifty thousand. If he does—and we decide to let the road go—I want Jeannie Magoffin to have a piece of it. A generous piece of it, I mean."

"That's okay with me," the tall man said. "If you hadn't brought it up, I'd have mentioned it . . . Let's go."

At the depot they found Jennings and Wheeler seated atop a packing box, enjoying the sunshine. In the office the telegraph receiver was tapping busily.

"Sounds like there was something coming through now," Rip said to them.

"About time—unless they're making a house to house canvass," Wheeler observed with his usual flippancy. "Jen and I have agreed to share whatever we get off the wire."

Con Hanrahan was in the office with Jeannie. He leaned out of the open window, two or three minutes later, and got Jennings' attention. "Message for you."

Jennings glanced at it quickly and looked puzzled. "I don't know whether this is the tip off or not. Listen: 'Colton, Ketchel and several others have just acquired Rocky Mountain

Short Line. No plans disclosed as yet. If they purchase Thunder River R.R. see possible hookup with Short Line. Get confirmation or denial. Want everything you can send.'"

Jennings reread the message carefully before handing it to Wheeler.

"What a pipe dream!" the latter jeered. "Simpson must have been three sheets in the winds when he got this off his chest. Coupling up the hard-luck little Short Line and the Thunder River narrow gauge! The Continental Divide and the Thunder River Range stand between them!"

"It may not be as crazy as you think," Jennings declared. "The Short Line's busted more men than all the rest of the standard gauge railroads in Colorado. Millions of dollars have been poured into the rat hole its been trying to punch through the Divide for the past seven or eight years. But that might be an asset; it's two-thirds of the way through. Colton's got money enough behind him to finish it."

"Where is the bore located?" Grumpy inquired.

"Under Spanish Peak. If it's ever completed it'll be better than five miles long. It will put the Short Line into Middle Park."

"And that will be just the same as putting it nowhere," Wheeler scoffed.

Rainbow had nothing to say; he felt he was learning just by listening.

"It would cost three or four million to finish that tunnel," Wheeler persisted. "The Short Line's in and out of twenty short tunnels between Denver and the Peak. They wouldn't have any picnic running across Middle Park, and then they'd still have the Thunder River Range staring them in the face. No, sir! It's a pipe dream!"

"Suppose we go in and have a look at the map," Rip suggested, finally.

Jeannie saw them coming and asked Con to let them in. Having taken the message off the wire, she was familiar with its contents and no little concerned. It had been a trying day for her. That the T.R. and N. was to continue to operate was a welcome reprieve, but she had not yet been able to adjust herself to the fact that it had a new owner. How the change was to affect her personally, she didn't know. She was aware of Grumpy's friendly interest and of Rip's too, for that matter. She took courage from it, and in far greater degree than she realized.

"Rainbow wants to look at the map, Miss Jeannie," Grumpy explained. "Do you mind?"

"Certainly not. If those letter files are in the way, I'll move them."

"Don't bother," said Rip. "I want to locate Spanish Peak."

"It's right here," she volunteered, putting her finger on the map. "It's about forty air-line miles northwest of Denver. I couldn't help overhearing what you gentlemen were saying outside." She moved her finger an inch or two. "This is Middle Park. If the Short Line was to be extended, with the idea of connecting with the T.R. and N., I should imagine the only practical way would be to swing around these twelve-thousand-foot peaks and thread its way up Long Valley to the headwaters of Priddy Creek and go over Mears Pass. Do you agree with me, Con?"

"I do; it's the best way there is. It'll burn up money. Some of it will cost fifty to seventy-five thousand dollars a mile."

"No trouble there. It's a low pass—not over eight thousand feet. Two percent grades would git you there. Wan of thim big Mallets would push over Mears Pass without raising a sweat. You'd need a couple miles of snow sheds to git your trains through in the winter."

"I'm afraid you'll have to pull in your horns, Wheeler," the tall man observed soberly. "That telegram is beginning to make a lot of sense . . . They finish the Spanish Peak tunnel, find a practicable way of reaching Mears Peak on two percent grades and it puts them right here in Painted Meadows. Once they have the Thunder River and Northern in the bag, they can coast down Ute Canyon and be off for Salt Lake."

"Another transcontinental, you mean?" Wheeler laughed skeptically. "We've got two of them. Where's the business going to come from for a third?"

"That's not my idea." Rainbow's tone had lost its velvety

edge. "You've got two major railroads running from Denver to Salt Lake, but they're all over the map before they get there. If one of them could cut off a couple hundred miles and straighten itself out, it'd get the business, wouldn't it?"

"Yeh. What's your point?"

"Look at the map and you'll see what I see. Forget about Lively. If a new road comes over Mears Pass it will hug the mountains to Chipeta. It's only about twenty-six miles from there to Revelation on the mainline of the Denver and Pacific. That cut-off would straighten things out for them, wouldn't it? It would shave a good two hundred miles from the Denver-Salt Lake run."

"Rip, you've hit the nail on the head!" Jennings exclaimed excitedly. "It's the right of way down Ute Canyon that Colton and Ketchel want! They've got to have it! It'll save them a couple million dollars!"

"They've got to have it if it's down the canyon they're going," Con spoke up. "You boys have seen it; you know there's no room for two roads."

"It's true!" Jeannie said, her voice unsteady. "My father always told me if one of the big roads ever wanted to go down the canyon they would have to come to him. Mr. Curry knew all about this. It explains why he was in Denver so often of late."

"Of course he knew," Grumpy muttered. "He was to git more out of it than his bankin' business and his ranch will ever be worth."

Wheeler was not ready to give in, but he said, "I don't want to be a dog in the manger about this. You may be right. If you are, Jen and I have one of the biggest stories that's broken in a long time. Tell me, Rip, what makes you think it's the Denver and Pacific who're after this little road?"

The tall man shrugged. "Maybe it's just a hunch. You told me Ketchel had been chief counsel for the D. and P. for years. I think you'll find he still is."

"I don't know," Wheeler declared dubiously. "If it's true, I'm surprised that Grumpy hasn't had an offer from him. Fifty thousand—a hundred thousand! It'd be small change, if they really want the right of way." He caught Grumpy looking very wise. "Say, have you had an offer?"

"Suppose you ask them," the little one returned craftily.

"So you did!" Wheeler threw up his hands. "That convinces me . . . Come on, Jen, let's see if we can't get a statement out of Ketchel and Colton!"

The partners sat down with Jeannie and Con. Grumpy told her that Rip now held an equal interest with himself in the road and she was to regard herself as their partner. She tried to thank them, but the little man cut her off.

"Let's not git our hopes up too high, Jeannie. It's some relief to know where you stand, even if it turns out to be on top of a case of dynamite. And dynamite is jest about what it is."

"Or worse," said Rainbow. His gray eyes were sober. "The Denver and Pacific is a multi-million-dollar corporation. They'll make us a series of offers for our rights in Ute Canyon. When they find that we know what we've got and can't be bought off for a song, they'll turn their wolf loose on us. We'll need support—plenty of it—and I believe we'll have it. How long we can buck them, I wouldn't attempt to say. But they'll know they've been in a fight before they grab the Thunder River and Northern and turn Lively into another ghost town."

CHAPTER 10

THE PARTNERS spent an hour with Jeannie, discussing the immediate requirements of the road. Con would have excused himself, but they asked him to stay.

"The first thing to do is pay up the back taxes," Rip said, in the course of their discussion. "We don't want to leave ourselves open in that direction. How about the roadbed, Con?"

"It's not too bad, Rainbow. We've got a little steel on hand. I could put in a new rail, here and there. There's an engine in the roundhouse that's better in some ways than the wan we're using. Me and Junie have been working on it in our spare time. A couple hundred dollars will put her in shape."

"We'll have money here by the middle of next week," Grumpy volunteered. "I reckon Con and the others have got some wages due. We'll take of that. How many men have you got cuttin' ties, Jeannie?"

"Five, at present."

"Wal, if there's money in it, why can't we put ten men

up there? You can sell all the ties you deliver in White River Junction, can't you?"

"There's been no question about that," she replied. "I've been selling to the Denver and Pacific. If we're going to be in a knockdown fight with them, they may refuse to do business with us. Of course there's the Midland. I believe they'll be glad to get them. If I haven't shipped more than a car or two a week, it's been only because I couldn't finance more; the checks are always thirty to sixty days coming through."

"That'll be all right now," Rip told her. "I think Grumpy's idea is a good one; if we can double up on the ties we ship, it'll come close to keeping us out of the red. I'd like to go up to the camp tomorrow and look things over. The doctor's agreed to take this bandage off my arm in the morning. It won't take long. I'll be ready to go about noon."

"Con will take you up," Jeannie said. "You'll find we've no worry about timber to be cut; there's plenty of it."

"That there is," Hanrahan agreed. "We'll use the handcar as far as the Y below Chipeta. From there, we'll have to hoof it; a man would break his back pumping that open-air Pullman up the tie-siding; the grade's so stiff we let the loaded cars run down on gravity. Wan of them got away from us onct and ended up down in the canyon. If we had another engine in service, we could use her up there."

"We'll have it," Rainbow assured him. "There won't be any splurging, but we'll do our level best to enable the Thunder River and Northern to pay its own way. It would be foolish to sit back and wait for Colton's crowd to make us an acceptable proposition. There's always the chance, too, that they may change their plans and go tooting off in some other direction and never hit Painted Meadows."

After toying with her pencil a moment, Jeannie looked up suddenly. "Do you really believe there is that chance, Rainbow?"

"No, I don't," he said, noting the anxiety in her eyes. "It's a possibility, that's all."

"You speak of an acceptable offer," she said. "Have you and Grumpy settled on something?"

"Not at all. They've offered us twenty-five thousand. They could afford to offer ten times that. But money alone won't satisfy us, and I don't believe it would satisfy you. You've fought hard to keep this corner of Colorado in touch with the rest of the State by rail. I know you'll never give up on that; you don't want to see Lively wither away to nothing."

"I certainly don't. But I'm not sure I follow you." Jeannie looked as puzzled as she sounded. "The town is here. It produces some business. Why should a new railroad leave it behind?"

"You know the record of Denver and Pacific," Rip pointed out. "It's become their policy to build their own towns. Their Land Department engineers that, and a pretty penny it's made them. There's business here, but they'll never build across the Meadows to get it; they'll line out for Ute Canyon. The best Lively would get would be a stub line, and I question that it would get even that. If any town is built in this valley, it well could be at Chipeta. It wouldn't surprise me if a deal for it hasn't been made already. That could be Mark Curry's piece of the pie."

Jeannie sighed. "I can believe that... You haven't met Bent, have you?"

"Not yet," the tall man acknowledged.

"I'm worried about him. When I left him at the courthouse, he told me he couldn't go on; that he'd have to break with his father."

"I should think he would," Grumpy observed testily. "He knows his old man tried to sell you out, and the valley, too. He looks to me like he could git ahead on his own."

"I'm sure he can," Jeannie agreed, pride in her voice. "But I don't want to see him cut off without a cent on my account."

"Yore account?" the little one questioned incredulously. "You know you didn't have nothin' to do with it. That was the rottenest part about this business—Curry trying to make out that he was gunnin' for you because he didn't want you and Bent goin' together... Oh, I've heard it!" he added as he saw Jeannie's eyes fill with embarrassment. "Forgit it!

Mark Curry's a dead letter around here, or he will be before we git through with him."

Noon-time came before they saw anything of Jennings and Wheeler.

"We wondered where you'd disappeared to," said Rip.

"We've been at the bank, firing questions at Miles Colton and his legal watchdog," Jennings informed him. "They're a hard pair to break down. They're arranging new financing for the Rocky Mountain Short Line, they admit. 'We're going to complete the Spanish Peak tunnel,' says Colton. 'If we had secured the Thunder River and Northern, it would have been to hold it for possible future development. But as to its being a Denver and Pacific move? Absurd! Nothing to it,' says he." Jennings' mocking laugh expressed what he thought about it.

In the same caustic vein, Wheeler said, "Ketchel tried to play coy with us, too. He couldn't explain why he had tagged along to help Colton pick up a worn out junkpile like the T. R. and N. I've interviewed him a couple of dozen times. He's usually ice-water, but he boiled over when I tried to pin him down on his connection with the Denver and Pacific. I couldn't get a yes or no out of him, so I ran a little bluff. I told him we had information in the office to the effect that he was still heading their legal staff. He threatened to sue us for libel if we printed any such statement." Jennings chuckled. "That told me what I wanted to know; when these big operators begin to squeal, you can be damn sure you're stepping on their toes."

"That cat's out of the bag," Wheeler declared, lighting a cigarette. "It's front page stuff. "We've got to thank you, Rainbow, for not letting us run away from it."

After dinner, they met Link.

"Bound for the depot ag'in, eh?" the old man hailed them. "Reckon it's headquarters from now on." He gave Rip a sly wink. "Jeannie'll have to clear a desk for you, Grump, so you'll feel at home. Reckon yo're a railroad president."

"By gum, I reckon I am!" the little man observed, with a wagging of his head. "I hadn't thought of that. In the future,

I hope you'll keep that in mind, Rip," he added, pulling down the corners of his mouth and pretending to be intrigued with his own importance. "When you speak to me, show me a little respect."

"I'll show you plenty of hard work," the tall man returned, not to be taken in for a moment.

Contrary to their expectations, the afternoon wore on without Colton or Ketchel getting in touch with them.

"Lettin' us stew in our own juice," Grumpy remarked.

"That's all right," Rainbow admonished him. "We can sit tight, too."

Jeannie left them in charge of the office for an hour. When she returned, young Bent Curry was with her. She made him acquainted with the partners. They gathered from her manner and Bent's that the latter's difficulty with his father had come to a head. That proved to be true.

"I couldn't take any more of it," Bent told them. "He'll have to go his way, and I'll go mine."

"Everyone we've talked to has had a good word to say for you," Grumpy said. "Is it a clean break with yore old man? Cut you off, I mean?"

Bent nodded. "He said I needn't expect a cent from him. But that's all right; I've got a little money of my own. I don't have to rush out looking for a job. I was telling Jeannie that the thing I'd like to do would be to get into this fight with you. I don't know what I can do to help, but there should be something."

"There will be," the tall man assured him. He was glad to have Bent's support. "If things go the way I imagine they will, we'll need all the help we can get. You couldn't do anything better for us, Bent, than to line up the stockmen on our side. I understand some of them are in debt to your father. That may hold them back. How do you think they'll feel about it?"

"I've talked to three or four already. Dutch Altmeyer's attitude is typical. The bank holds a mortgage on his ranch, but as Dutch says, how's he going to pay it off if Lively loses the railroad? The value of his place will be cut in two. Lem Spade and Uncle Joe Corbett feel about the same."

"Good!" Rainbow exclaimed. "You get them lined up, Bent. Next week, we'll get together with them and the leading merchants in town, like Louie Bannerman, and see if we can't get some support organized."

"Fine!" Bent agreed. "I'll move my stuff into town to-morrow and keep in touch with you. Where will you hold the meeting?"

"We better hold it right here in Lively. I'll speak to Bannerman. If he's agreeable, we'll have it in his store."

In spite of its overtone of trouble ahead, Jeannie took heart from Rainbow's plans. The partners were pleased to see her her smiling confident self again.

On Rip's advice, he and Grumpy kept away from the hotel for the rest of the day. "If Colton or Ketchel have anything to say, let them look us up."

They were in Link's office at the jail that evening, seated with him and Greenwood and the two officers from Wyoming, when Ketchel appeared and called them outside.

"I'd like to go to the hotel and sit down with you for a few minutes and talk things over," he said.

"We haven't anything to say that can't be said here," Rip demurred. "What's on your mind?"

"I'm afraid you gentlemen are barking up the wrong tree." The lawyer's suavity had faded quickly. "You think you know what we want and that all you have to do is sit back and we'll make you one offer after another until you get your price. That doesn't happen to be the case. We've had two men on Moran Mountain all winter—competent engineers. They haven't driven a stake, but they've had their eyes open. We know we can come over Mears Pass and reach Ute Canyon without ever touching the Painted Meadows."

"But that won't take you down the canyon," Grumpy averred.

"Not at the river level. We can stay high above it and blast out a roadbed. And we'll do it rather than be held up for some preposterous sum for what you've got."

"Then we all know where we stand," Rainbow said evenly. "Suppose we let it go at that."

The manner in which the partners dissembled their surprise at learning that the two "uranium" prospectors were engineers in the employ of Denver and Pacific, made Ketchel realize he wasn't dealing with novices in this game of give and take.

"Mr. Colton and I are leaving for Denver in the morning," said he. "I'll make you a final offer. You can have the rest of the night to think it over. We'll give you fifty thousand dollars for the Thunder River and Northern."

"It doesn't interest us, Mr. Ketchel," Rainbow was quietly emphatic about it. "Any offer that would appeal to us would have to include certain guarantees beyond the amount of money we received."

"For instance?" Ketchel queried.

"That you run your rails through Lively and make the town more than a whistle stop."

Ketchel dismissed it with a wave of his hand. "I agree with you that we are wasting our time. There's no need to say anything further—unless it is to admit that I admire your spunk a great deal more than your judgment. I'll bid you good evening, gentlemen."

Grumpy looked at Rainbow as they stood there alone, a slightly bewildered look on his leathery face. "Fifty thousand," he muttered. "You turned it down without batting an eyelash!"

"Don't tell me you'd have accepted, Grump."

"No! But fifty thousand bucks—that's a heap of money. We work all year, and if we knock down fifteen thousand, we figger we're doin' all right. But these big shots talk about fifty thousand as though it was chicken feed. And yet they're penny pinchers. Curry could have had the road for ten thousand if he'd offered it to Jeannie . . . What do you figger their next move will be?"

"They'll make us trouble of some sort—something they calculate will soften us up, and then we'll get another offer from them. We better not be taken in another time the way those two lads down in Chipeta pulled the wool over our eyes. Looking for uranium! I'll remember that!"

In the morning, Morgan and Tovey, shackled together, were led to the train. The partners walked down with Greenwood and Link. Ketchel and Colton were already seated in the day coach. The reporters were on the platform. They shook hands with Rip and Grumpy.

"Better keep an eye on the Denver papers," Wheeler suggested. "If you happen to hit town, look us up."

With the departure of the train, Lively seemed rather deserted. That afternoon saw the partners and Con on their way to the camp. The doctor had found Rip's arm nearly healed, but the tall man favored it. Still, one good arm was all he needed to help pump the handcar.

It didn't take them long to reach the Y below Chipeta. The three-mile hike to the camp was a stiff one. Rainbow was particularly interested in sizing up the men who were employed there and talking to Jim Flynn, the foreman. Flynn proved to be a husky, voluble Irishman. Con started to acquaint him with what had occurred the previous day, only to find that everyone in camp was already up-to-date on it.

"O'Malley's lad rode into camp last evening," Flynn told him. "He had all the news."

The partners had begun to realize that Jeannie's first requirement in a man she employed seemed to be that he be an Irishman.

"We're going to try to double the number of ties we're shipping," Rainbow told the foreman. "You'll need a bigger gang up here. Can you put your hand on some experienced men?"

"Aisy enough," big Jim answered. "There's some of thim mackerel snatchers from County Mayo down in White River Junction who know how to use the long saw and the adz."

"We don't want any Denver and Pacific spies in this camp," Rainbow said bluntly. "There's a fight coming, and we want to be sure we can count on your gang."

"Bejabbers, if it's a fight I can promise them boys I got in mind, they'll come running!" Flynn declared with a hearty chuckle. "I'll sell my soul on it, they got no love for D. and P."

"Well, you knock off work on Monday and go down to the Junction," Rip told him. "Hire half a dozen men. There'll be no more waiting for wages; you'll be paid on the dot."

"Flag the down train at Chipeta," Con instructed the big fellow. "I'll tell the boys to be looking for you."

The method by which the loaded cars were moved down the steep grade interested the partners.

"Shure it's dangerous," Con admitted, "but save for the one mishap I told you about, we've never had an accident. Whin the cars are ready to go, I come up. The trick is not to let them git to rolling too fast. A few yards at a time— stop—and then take another bite. That's how it's done."

When they reached the Y Rip suggested that they have a look around Chipeta. "We won't find those would-be uranium prospectors there. You can be sure word was got to them to clear out, or Ketchel wouldn't have let that cat out of the bag last night. They undoubtedly flagged the down train this morning."

As he predicted, they found the cabin, which the men had occupied so long, deserted. There were signs that they had left hurriedly.

"They didn't bother to dump the waste basket," Grumpy observed.

"Suppose we do it," said Rainbow. "Dump it on the table. We may find a notation or two that will interest us."

That proved to be an understatement. Much of the paper litter held only unintelligible notations, but they found enough to piece out what appeared to be the route the new road would take, after coming over Mears Pass.

"Looks like you figgered it right," Con declared. "Lively's got no place in their plans, Rainbow."

"I think that's plain enough," the tall man agreed. "Some of these scraps lead me to believe that Chipeta has been replotted—streets laid out. Look at this one. This square here is even marked depot."

Though Grumpy confessed that he wasn't smart enough

to understand many of the strange symbols and problems the engineers had used in figuring out grades and degrees of curvature, he was just as deeply interested in the search as Rip. In fact, it so engrossed them that they were not aware that they were being watched until a rough-looking individual tapped on the window. As their attention was drawn in that direction, the door opened and a burly giant, beside whom Jim Flynn would have looked small, burst in on them, a pick handle clutched in his ham-like fist. His hair was a brick red, and so was the several-days' growth of wiry bristles that decorated his iron jaw. Behind his mounds of fat, his blue eyes flamed menacingly as he saw what the partners and Con were doing.

"Snoopin', eh?" he roared. "I figgered yuh might be! Yuh'll git outa here now or git yore heads busted! And you'll leave them papers on the table!"

"Wait a minute, Shag!" Con protested. "We got as much right here as you have. Since the mining company wint bust, no wan claims this camp."

"Is that so?" the red-haired giant flung back angrily. He had five men, cut to his own pattern, waiting to rush in at his call. "This camp has been bought up. It's private property. Me and my boys are here to see that there's no trespassin' er usin' a match. You heard me tell yuh to git out. Now git!"

Rip was not to be cowed. "You know this man, Con?"

"Shag Kissick? Shure I know him. Him and his bully boys have been busting heads for the D. and P. for years. They got here in a hurry. Brought up to the lower end of the canyon by wagon and hoofed it up the gorge."

"Mebbe he got here a little too quick," Grumpy purred. His hand had found his gun. Unhurried, he whipped it out. "I'm jest a little squirt, Kissick, but this pea-shooter sorta evens things up. Drop that pick handle! If yore friend outside tries to take a hand in this, I'll drop you . . . Gather up them papers, Rip. We'll take 'em with us for whatever they may be worth."

It had been their intention to flag the north-bound train

and ride back to Lively. The little one saw no reason to change their plans.

"We'll march our friend down to the tracks with us," he said. "He'll be a dead pigeon—if there's any snipin' from the rest of his gang ... That plain, Kissick?"

"Yeh!" Shag snarled in his beard. "There'll be another time, I reckon!"

"I hope so!" Grumpy snapped. "I don't like yore looks or yore smell!"

CHAPTER 11

RAINBOW REGARDED the presence in Chipeta of Shag Kissick and his rowdies as having such serious implications that he felt it was necessary to discuss it freely with Jeannie, and at once.

"I want you to sit in on it," he told Con. "And I want Bent there, too. If he isn't at the depot, we'll send for him."

Bent was on hand when the train pulled in. Rip spoke to him briefly, telling him what had happened.

"I expected something of the sort," Bent said. "I didn't expect it quite so soon. We can run them out, Rip. I can round up a dozen men and we can go down tonight."

"We'll have to be sure of our ground before we try anything like that," the tall man replied. "If the land has been sold, and they're acting for the owner, they have a legal right to be there. We won't help ourselves any by stepping outside the law. With a battery of high-priced lawyers to throw at us, the Denver and Pacific will be waiting for us to do that very thing. As soon as Jeannie is free, we'll talk it over with her."

Though she could not help being alarmed by the news, she managed to take it calmly.

Rainbow repeated what he had said to Bent. "I'd like nothing better than to go down there and run them out; but I know that would be a mistake. We'll have to watch them. If they molest our trains or destroy our property, we'll have an excuse for going after them."

"That's what they're there to do, Rip. You know it," Grumpy declared soberly. "What other reason could there be?"

"To protect their surveyors, who won't be long in showing up. At least that was Colton's idea when he ordered them sent to Chipeta. He was so sure at that time that he would get the T. R. and N. that he didn't hesitate. It's the only way they could have had time to get up from White River Junction."

They spent an hour trying to piece together the bits of information to be gathered from the scraps of paper they had found in the cabin.

"It's plain enough," Bent declared. "They don't intend to come into Lively."

"I could have told you that from the way Ketchel froze up when we put it to him last night," Grumpy stated. "That's something for you to keep in mind, Bent, when you make the rounds of the valley on Monday."

"You couldn't have a stronger argument for getting your Painted Meadows cowmen together for a meeting," Rip told him. "It'll be Monday before we can get into the courthouse and have a look at the records. If that property has changed hands, a deed will have to be recorded. I'll attend to that."

"Why don't we see Bannerman this evenin' and sound him out?" the little man asked. "If he's agreeable, we can cover the town tonight and hit the valley with Bent tomorrow—we've still got Bullard's broncs. It'll give us a chance to git acquainted, and it'll save time. We can hold the meetin' Monday night."

Rainbow was agreeable. Being Saturday, the stores were open late. They saw Louie and he liked their idea so well that he put on his hat and called on his fellow merchants with them.

"You won't have any trouble lining up Dutch and Lem Spade and the rest of them," he predicted. "Tell them to show up at my store Monday evening, at eight. Mark Curry ain't doing no more strutting. Whether you know it or not, the feeling against him is getting worse by the hour. When news of what's in the wind down at Chipeta gets around, I wouldn't want to be in his boots."

"Curry's the least of our worries," said Grumpy. "He's jest the errand boy for that Denver crowd."

Sunday dawned clear and warm. Up in the San Cristobals and the Thunder River Range, the snow fields were beginning their annual retreat.

"This is fine!" Grumpy declared exuberantly, as Rip and he made their way back to Link's barn, where Bent was already waiting for them. "We're gittin' into May; the weather ought to hold good right into summer."

They made their first stop at Dutch Altmeyer's ranch. Dutch didn't have to be persuaded. "By golly, I'll be there with bells on," he told them. They met with an equally enthusiastic reception from Lem Spade and Corbett. Only once during the course of the day were they unable to get a promise of support.

"Ben Small couldn't be much help to us in any event," Bent asserted, as they turned back to town. "He's in bad health. His little spread's been running down for a couple of years."

"We did all right," said Grumpy. "We'll have a crowd on hand tomorrow night. I only hope you have some luck at the courthouse, Rip. But you know a deed ain't always recorded promptly. A clerk gits his palm greased and he can cover up for a time."

Rainbow nodded. "I know it. Who will I have to see, Bent?"

"Molly Hawkins. She's been county clerk for years. You needn't worry about that old girl holding anything back; she's strictly honest."

Monday morning brought the partners a long letter from their good friend Judge Carver, at Black Forks, Wyoming, enclosing the certified check they had requested. Also, by express, they received the personal effects they had left in Salt Creek.

"We can settle down and make ourselves to home now," said Grumpy. "While yo're in the courthouse, I'll step into Curry's bank and open an account. I don't imagine he'll be glad to see me."

At the bank, the cashier waited on him. Curry sat at his desk, doing his best not to notice the little one. Grumpy returned the banker's disregard with interest, when he stalked out.

An hour passed before he saw Rainbow coming. The tall man's eyes were inscrutable as usual, but his step had a bounce that said he had been successful.

"You found it, eh?" Grumpy queried.

"Yeh! Marcus Curry owns it. Bought it a couple months ago. Come along; we're going to see Link. He can do us a little favor."

They found the old man in his office. Rip told him about the gang that had moved into Chipeta.

"This is the first I heard of it," the sheriff declared. "I'll go down there and see what's what."

"They may be within their rights, Link. I've just come from the courthouse; Marcus Curry is now the owner of record on the Chipeta property. Shag Kissick and his men may be there with Curry's permission. Would you mind putting the matter up to him?"

"Not at all! I'm interested in any bunch of men who move into my jurisdiction and can't give a good account for their presence. You wait here; I'll see Mark and git a yes or no out of him!"

Link wasn't gone long. He came back scowling.

"Curry says they're there to guard the old buildin's. I asked him who's payin' their wages. He wouldn't give me an answer. Wanted to know what I was up to. By Joe, I told him!

I warned him if they was planted there to make trouble for Jeannie's road, I'd jug 'em, the first move they made!"

"That gives us all the ammunition we need," Grumpy averred. "It knocks the guesswork out of it. We can talk facts tonight."

"Yo're holdin' a meetin', I understand," the old man observed.

Rip said yes. "You're welcome, Link. We didn't ask you to attend because we thought you might feel your official position wouldn't permit you to be present."

Link thought it over for a moment or two. "I better keep away," he decided. "But jest between us, you've got my support. That don't mean I'm hidin' behind my badge; I know what this community is up against; Painted Meadows and Lively don't mean a thing to that big-money crowd in Denver. If we git a break, we'll have you boys to thank for it."

The evening train brought Saturday's Denver papers. Front page headlines shrieked the news that the Denver and Pacific and Rocky Mountain Short Line were now one and the same; that with the completion of the Spanish Peak Tunnel, new construction would carry the rails across Middle Park and the Thunder River Range and cut into the parent company's mainline, somewhere west of White River Junction, a cut-off that would save several hundred miles and give Denver what it always had wanted, a direct east and west line to Salt Lake City and the Coast.

Obviously, the sleuthing of newsmen in the capital had unearthed facts which could not be denied. There were howls of dismay from certain towns in the southern part of the State who stood to lose their standing as division points, with the straightening out of D. and P.

"By grab, here's our picture!" Grumpy exclaimed. "And Wheeler's story of the sale of the Thunder River and Northern! Anythin' about it in the sheet yo're readin'?

"Yeh, it's all here, under Jennings's by-line."

They had grabbed the papers the moment they came off the train and hurried into the depot with them.

"Are the two of you going to devour every line before I

get a glance to see what they say?" Jeannie inquired, with a chiding frown.

"I'm sorry," said Rainbow. "Here, sit down and read it aloud."

It took her some time to read the long accounts in the two papers.

"Jeannie, do you see anything about Morgan and Tovey?" the little one questioned.

After turning the pages, she found an account of the capture of the bandits on page five.

"Here's half a column," she said. "Shall I read it to you?"

"Go ahead," the partners chorused.

"It ain't much of a story, considerin' the trouble them reporters went to to git it," Grumpy complained, when she had finished.

"Got crowded out by this railroad stuff," Rip told him. "And just as well. All this newspaper fanfare confirms what we believed to be the case, but we haven't learned anything new. Frankly, I'd have been surprised if we had. The three of us knew we had locked horns with one of the most powerful corporations in Colorado. The sooner we get used to the idea, the better."

Jeannie nodded a silent acceptance of that fact. After a moment or two, she said, "How long will your meeting at Bannerman's last?"

"An hour, I imagine," Rip answered. "We'll see that Bent drops around to your house afterwards. I know you'll be anxious to hear what we accomplished."

"I'll appreciate it, Rainbow." Her mouth lost its pretty curve and her young face was suddenly grave. "It isn't going to be easy for Bent—I mean in regard to his father. There's bound to be talk against Marcus Curry."

"No avoidin' that," the little man agreed emphatically. "If the old skinflint had shot square with the boy and you, this whole thing could have been worked out and nobody would have got hurt. The chips are down now, and I reckon Bent knows it . . . Have you seen him today?"

"This morning, before he left for the ranch. He expected

to be back in town about now. He's bringing his things in.
He's going to live with the Deans, for the present. His mother
was a Dean . . . Take the papers with you, Grumpy; I'll stop
at Little Phil's on the way home and get some copies for
myself."

After supper the partners sat upstairs in their room, with
Grumpy immersed in the newspapers, his boots off, as usual.
He finally put the papers down and removed his glasses.

"I can't believe we're in this," he muttered, a far-away
look in his eye. "The whole dang thing seems like a dream."

"Well, it was you, my fine friend, who got us into it,"
Rainbow reminded him tartly. "Don't come around trying to
lock the barn door now."

"Who is?" the little one snapped. "I know we're in this
up to our necks—and it's okay with me. I was jest tryin' to
say if you'd told me ten days ago that this was where we was
goin' to end up, I'd have said you was crazy."

"That I can agree with," said Rip. "Pull on your boots and
we'll go down the street to Louie's."

They found three or four men on hand already. Others
continued to arrive, Bent Curry among them, and by eight
o'clock, over thirty were present. Louie got their attention
and called the impromptu meeting to order.

"I'll make this short," he said. "You know why we're here
and what we're up against. Most of you have read the evening
papers from Denver. I understand there's been other devel-
opments during the day. I'll let Ripley do the talking."

On Saturday evening, the partners had spoken freely of
what they had run into at Chipeta, and again on the previous
day during their ride around the valley. What Rainbow had
learned at the courthouse that morning, confirmed in large
part what they had been saying. He began by stating what
his investigation had disclosed.

"The dirty crook!" Dutch exploded. "Curry's been workin'
on this for months! Bought three hundred acres, you say. I
bet he got it for a song. That land's worthless; you can't grow
nothin' on it!"

"He ain't aiming to grow anything on it," Louie Bannerman spoke up. "He's figuring to lay out a town down there and sell it to us by the foot. If he gets away with it, property in Lively won't be worth a nickel!"

Lem Spade, dark and cadaverous-looking, had his say. He was accounted a man of parts, having been the first stockman to run cattle in the Painted Meadows.

"He won't get away with it if I know it! I can see what his game is, plain enough! Instead of stickin' my money in his bank, whenever I had any to spare, I bought real estate here in town. You've done the same, Uncle Joe. If values go to hell in Lively, our savings are goin' down the drain!"

"That's bound to happen," Uncle Joe Corbett agreed. "I've had it in mind ever since Mark Curry put the narrow gauge up for sale." He was a wisp of a man, stoop shouldered and so washed out that he appeared to have one foot in the grave. But he had looked the same for twenty years.

"I was readin' the papers at the hotel before I came over," he continued. "I reckon a man can hear more rumors and wild talk in Colorado than any place on earth. But this ain't talk; we got somethin' comin' at us. It ain't only the little property I got in town that's goin' to be knocked into a cocked hat; it means I'll have nine, ten miles further to drive my beef, to do business at the courthouse, or just to come in for a sack of flour." He looked around the store at his fellow ranchers. "That goes for every one of you. I'm not goin' to take this lyin' down, and I told Ripley and his pardner so yesterday. If I thought stringin' up Mark Curry would be a way out, I'd be in favor of it. But that won't stop it; it's got beyond that. He's cut the ground out from under us, but it won't do no good to call him names."

There was a wide difference of opinion as to that, and right and left men cursed Curry and called him a scheming, double-dealing coyote.

"Even his own son—his own flesh and blood—can't stand him!" Lem Spade burst out, his voice rising above the tumult. "Mark Curry's a low-down, no account crook! I got more use for a hoss thief!"

There was movement at the door. The several men standing

there were brushed aside and Marcus Curry stalked in, his
jaw set. He received a blistering reception.

"Open the door and throw him out!" someone cried.

Others took it up.

"You better listen to what I've got to say!" Curry roared.
"You let a couple strangers come to town and make you
believe black is white! I don't care what you think of me,
but if you'll give me your attention, maybe I can open your
eyes."

The crowd stilled its clamor.

"For years I've dreamed of giving Painted Meadows a real
railroad," he went on. "You've seen the Thunder River and
Northern going from bad to worse—one train in and one out
a day. And what trains! Broken down equipment! A roadbed
that's as crooked as a camel's back! Two hours to get us to
White River Junction!" His tone eloquently expressed what
he thought about all this. "It doesn't require any brains to
see that it's been holding this valley back—hurting every
one of us. You may think the Denver and Pacific suddenly
got the idea of building this way. That's not true; it was my
idea, and I'm proud of it. I've spent my money and my time
inducing them to buy the Rocky Mountain Short Line and
making the cut-off to Revelation. It'll be the making of Painted
Meadows."

"What about Chipeta?" Dutch Altmeyer demanded scornfully. "You've been busy down there, ain't you?"

"I bought the land," Curry admitted readily. "It's a fine
town-site. Right on the river. That means water for irrigation
and for all future needs. We'll have a half dozen trains a day.
We can be in Denver in three hours."

The partners could see that some of the crowd were wav-
ering.

"You ain't sayin' anythin' about what's to become of
Lively," Lem Spade jerked out. "What do you intend to do—
have the grass growing out there in the main street?"

"There'll be some changes," Curry had to acknowledge.
"This talk of it becoming a ghost town is ridiculous."

"But Chipeta will git the play—and you own it!" Lem persisted. "How much you askin' for a fifty-foot lot?"

That did it. Curry tried to turn the question, but he couldn't get away from it. "I—I don't intend to gouge anyone!" he protested to no avail. "The railroad company will plan the town and do everything to encourage its growth."

"Oh, I see!" Spade shot back, thoroughly enraged. "Yo're goin' to turn it over to their Land Department when the time is ripe! . . . Wal, damn you, Curry, you've had yore say. Now git outa here!"

A surreptitious hand plucked an egg out of a bushel basket and heaved it at the banker. It missed its mark and splattered on the floor. It convinced Curry. Snorting his defiance and calling them fools, he marched out.

"I guess we can go on now," said Rip. "Mr. Curry claimed that my partner and I have been trying to make you believe black is white. You're evidently not as color blind as he thinks."

The crowd chuckled. When it quieted, the discussion continued for half an hour, with suggestions that some appeal be made to the courts.

"I don't see how the law can help us," said Rainbow. "We've got limited funds. You can't fight a greedy, million-dollar corporation that way and win."

"Wal, what is it you want of us, Ripley?" Lem Spade asked. "It ain't money, you say."

"No, we don't want money. It'll be enough for us if we can count on your moral support—plus the assurance that if we need help—and I mean men—that you'll come running."

"You've got it!" Spade declared. "Say the word, and me and my crew will be right there!"

The others said as much. The meeting broke up, but many stood around, talking, and it was getting on toward ten o'clock before the partners found themselves alone with Bent.

"We promised Jeannie we'd send you around to report on what took place," said Rip. "It's late. You better be on your way."

"Is there anything in particular you want me to tell her, Rip?"

"Just tell her that these people are standing with us—that we can put a hundred men in Ute Canyon if we have to."

CHAPTER 12

Jim Flynn had brought back from White River Junction the needed reinforcements for his tie-cutting gang. Con Hanrahan came down from the camp on Tuesday to report that the work was being speeded up.

"We'll need a second engine for shure now," he told the partners and Jeannie. "It won't take Junie and me long to finish putting the new flues in Number 3, once they git here."

"They should come up this evening," said Jeannie. "I ordered them by wire."

"If they do, we'll have Number 3 perking by the middle of the week. If it's okay with you, I'll put her on the run to the Junction and leave Number 2 in the shed for a day or so and do some work on her."

Jeannie turned to the partners with a questioning glance.

"Let's have this understood," said Rip; "you're operating the road. You don't have to refer anything of this nature to us. We don't pretend to know anything about railroading."

"That's right," Grumpy agreed.

"Very well," she acknowledged, with a smile. "You go

ahead, Con. You've always had a free hand in the past, and I want you to have it now. You know every nut and bolt on the road. You are just about the T.R. and N."

The lean, rawboned superintendent gave the partners a wink. "You see how she gits around me with her blarney. I understand our friend Marcus Curry has quite a different opinion of my labors. The roadbed's as crooked as a camel's back, says he. Well, I can give him the lie on that; a camel has humps, but there's nothing crooked about its back."

"That's more'n you can say for *his* back," Grumpy observed pointedly. "When Number 3 goes into service, you'll need another engine crew, won't you, Con?"

"Not for the work on the tie spur. I can run her, with wan of Jim Flynn's boys to keep steam up."

Link Easter rode up to the depot as they sat in the office. Leaving his horse at the rack, he burst in on them with a good morning for Jeannie and a nod for the rest. It was easily seen that he had something on his mind. He enlightened them at once.

"I saw Bent Curry, with a rifle in his saddle boot, sneakin' out of town an hour ago and headin' south. Are you boys sendin' him down to keep cases on that bunch at Chipeta?"

"He's going to spend some time on Moran Mountain," Rip admitted. "Anything wrong with that?"

"There's plenty wrong with it," Link declared thinly. "That bunch is in Chipeta for no good purpose. If they spot the boy, they'll likely take a pot shot at him."

"Yo're underestimatin' the lad," Grumpy protested. "Bent can take care of himself. He's not down there to have a run in with them. He's there to keep an eye on 'em and see what he can see."

"Hellsfire!" the old man snorted, "That's enough to spell trouble! Those gents ain't goin' to like the idea of havin' someone pussy-footin' around that mountain with a rifle under his leg. You could have left 'em to me. I'm headin' for Chipeta now."

"I'm glad you are," said Rainbow. "You won't see anything of Bent—unless you go looking for him. If you could stay down there, Link, it would take care of the situation; but you've got other duties . . . Just what is it you're objecting to? Curry doesn't own the mountain. You wouldn't want Bent to go unarmed, would you?"

"No! A man's armed if he's packin' a .45. It's that rifle I don't like. And I don't think you shoulda sent him alone. You boys are experienced. I wouldn't think twicest about it if you was meetin' up with him."

"Wal, mebbe that's the idea," came from Grumpy. "You jest keep yore rompers on, Link; we ain't figgerin' on takin' the law into our own hands jest yet. When we git ready to do some shootin', we'll send you an invitation. What's eatin' you—bustin' in here like this and scarin' Jeannie?"

Link was apologetic at once. "I didn't calculate to do that." He turned to her. "Jeannie, you forgit what I said. I know Bent's goin' to git into this scrap up to his neck—and rightly so. The only reason I got het up was becuz I don't want him to stub his toe—both for his account and yores."

"You haven't frightened me," she reassured him. She gave his arm an affectionate pat. "He'll be all right. Bent may be young, but he's older than his years. He gave a good account of himself on the ranch."

"He did! He shore did!" Link's attention shifted to Rainbow. "When are you and the little fella goin' down?"

"Sometime tomorrow."

"Okay! You look me up this evenin'. I'll let you know how I make out with Shag Kissick."

Without further ado, he got on his horse and rode off. The partners watched him from the window. They turned back finally to find Jeannie waiting for them.

"What was behind all that?" she demanded. "Link isn't in the habit of getting excited without a reason."

"I can't tell you why," said Rip, "but I can guess."

"Well?"

"That Link was only talking around the bush. I believe he thinks our first move may be to set fire to Chipeta, and that we sent Bent down to do it, while we show ourselves here in town so we can come up with an alibi. You know there's nothing to that. We hadn't intended riding down tomorrow, but we'll have to do it now."

Jeannie thought it over for several moments. "I hope you're right," she murmured. "It would be easy to touch a match to those old buildings, wouldn't it? If the wind was blowing in the right direction, Chipeta would be gone in an hour."

"No question about that." Rainbow's eyes were guileless, but he was aware of the trap she had spread for him. "I imagine Shag and his friends would be discommoded some; the nights are still cold. But driving them out into the open would be all a fire would accomplish."

It satisfied Jeannie, and she went back to work with her mind easy.

The partners saw Link that evening. The old man had a lot to say but they found nothing of importance in it until the very end, when he told them that Kissick claimed he had tried to flag the down train that morning and it had run by him.

"You wouldn't think a low brow like him would have brains enough in his thick skull to figger out that he can make you stop. He says you been stoppin' there on flag right along; that the last printed schedule the road filed shows Chipeta as a flag stop, and he'll make you stop. They're runnin' out of grub, he tells me."

"I'd like to see him make us stop!" Grumpy declared heatedly. "Does he think we're goin' to feed his camp and bring in material and men for him to raise hell with us?"

"You better speak to Jeannie about this," Link advised. "The T.R. and N. is a common carrier, operatin' under the State Railroad Act; I reckon things like that is covered in the charter Dave Magoffin got years ago."

"We better hire ourselves a lawyer and put it up to him," Rainbow suggested. "Can you recommend a good man, Link?"

"Why, Henry Purcell has always looked after any legal work Jeannie's had done. Hank drinks too much; but he knows the law. Put it up to Jeannie; she'll git an opinion from him." His shrewd eyes shifted from Rip to Grumpy and back. "I didn't see nothin' of Bent Curry."

"I told you you wouldn't unless you went looking for him," the tall man reminded him. "He's up on the mountain with a pair of binoculars, and he'll stay there. If there's a big fire in Chipeta, it won't be of our doing. You git that straight, Link. I don't like the idea of helping the Denver and Pacific to move in right under our noses any better than Grumpy does. But if we have to give them flag service at Chipeta, we'll do it; I don't believe they can make us reopen that boarded-up depot and keep an agent there, no matter how much material they ship in. If we have to, we'll haul it to Lively and make them freight it out from here."

"Of course—you could pull down the Chipeta depot and file a new schedule with the Railroad Commission," Link suggested slyly.

Rip eyed him with an obscure interest for a moment. "You mean that's what you're afraid we'll do. You've been beating around the bush all day, Link. You've heard something—or know something—that you're holding back on us. What is it?"

Link threw up his hands. "By Joe, do you have to push me into a corner? I hear some things I ain't supposed to hear. I'll tell you this much: if anythin' goes wrong at Chipeta— fire—refusal to stop on flag or to put a car of freight on the sidin'—yo're goin' to be in trouble. The T.R. and N. has to cross the Denver and Pacific to git into White River Junction. Wal, it won't git there. That'll be their answer. Find out what yore legal rights are, but don't depend on 'em to see you through. Yo're dealin' with an outfit that'll use the law whenever it's on their side and who won't give a damn for it when it's ag'in 'em."

The partners didn't press him further. Obviously what the sheriff had told them came either directly or indirectly from Curry. It kept them awake for several hours.

"Say, this proposition works two ways!" the little one rapped out, rousing himself from his scowling cogitation. "There's a hundred tricks they can pull to keep us out of the Junction; but if they do, how are they goin' to git any freight to Chipeta? And that'll be the important item. They'll bust their necks to git the cut-off completed before winter sets in. They won't be able to do it if the work's all done from the railhead at Spanish Peak, or even if they drive up this way from Revelation. The snow's flyin' in these mountains by late September."

"It's a bluff," said Rip. "I've thought so from the first. Curry let the tale slip to Link deliberately, being sure it would be passed on to us. When Colton and Ketchel were here, I don't doubt that they discussed this matter and many others with him. If they had come to a decision and given Curry the authority to speak for the D. and P., he'd have looked us up and laid it on the line."

"If it's a bluff, let's call it, Rip."

The tall man shook his head. "I don't think we can afford to. In any event, we'll wait until Jeannie sees her lawyer."

Purcell's opinion was disappointing.

"We can't be compelled to maintain an agent at Chipeta, he said," Jeannie advised the partners. "But as for accepting freight, he thinks we better do it. The siding is there, he says, and if the Denver and Pacific appeals to the Commission, we'll find it loaded against us."

"I reckon he advised you to stop there on flag," said Grumpy.

Jeannie nodded. "He was very positive about that. But he agrees with you, Rainbow, that no attempt will be made to keep us out of the Junction as long as the T.R. and N. can be of any use to them. I think I better wire Pop, at the Junction, to answer any flag he gets at Chipeta."

"I would," Rip told her. "It's almost noon. We'll get a bite to eat before we pull out for Moran Mountain. Bent may have something to tell us."

"It's knucklin' under 'em," Grumpy grumbled, as he and Rip left the depot. "They'll make the most of it."

Rainbow could only agree with him. "But," he added, "I prefer that to going to a lot of legal expense only to be knocked down in the end. We'll find plenty ways to make life miserable for that crowd as we go along. You wait; their shoe will begin to pinch long before they get over Mears Pass."

That afternoon, as they approached from the east, Bent spotted them, with the aid of his binoculars, before they started climbing from the flat-lands. Realizing they were looking for him, he took the trail down the wooded shoulder of the mountain. He had nothing startling to report.

"I watched them through the glasses all yesterday and again today," he told the partners. "I counted six of them, altogether. Half of them are living in one cabin, the rest are bunking in the shack next door. They barely stir. They come out and sun themselves for an hour and then drift back inside. I saw one of them go down to the river yesterday and try to catch some trout. He didn't have any luck and he gave up before long. He'd just got back when Link showed up. What was the old man doing down here?"

Rainbow told him what he and the little one believed was the sheriff's reason for making the trip. Bent was skeptical until he heard the whole story.

"Did they try to flag the down train this mornin'?" Grumpy asked.

"They sure did," Bent told him, with a laugh. "Dennis rattled through Chipeta without giving them a tumble. They shook their fists at him. I could hear them cursing, way up the mountain. Now you're going to stop for them, eh?"

"Yeh," said Rip. "You haven't been close enough to hear what they were saying?"

"I slipped down last evening, after dark. The big fellow, Kissick, and another one of them, took a stroll up the tie spur. I could hear their voices as they went up the grade."

"How long were they gone?"

"About an hour."

"They went up to look the camp over," Grumpy asserted. "Wal, they'll have their ears pinned back if they tangle with the gang Jim Flynn's got up there now. That'd be a ruckus I'd pay money to see."

"Flynn and his men can handle them, unless they're caught by surprise," Rainbow observed. "We better tell Con tomorrow to tip them off that they may have company some night.

... You mind sticking it out here another day or two, Bent? We brought some grub along for you."

"I'll be glad to stay, Rip. If I see anything that I think you ought to know, I'll light out for Lively in a hurry . . . How's Jeannie?"

"She's fine. She's queried the Midland and the Denver and Pacific about the ties. She thought she'd have an answer by the time we got back. Chances are the D. and P. will not be inclined to do any more business with her. There's no point in paying men wages to cut and dress ties if you can't find a market for them."

It was after five when he and the little one got back to town. They found Jeannie sorely perplexed.

"We needn't worry about disposing of our ties," she told them. "The Midland will take a carload a week, and get this— the Denver and Pacific will take all we can deliver."

"You don't mean it!" Rip exclaimed. "What's the catch?"

"They're to be delivered on the siding at Chipeta. They'll have men there to unload them as fast as they're received."

Grumpy's lined face turned a choleric purple. "Great day in the mornin'!" he exploded. "What are we supposed to do—dig our own grave? If we—"

"Wait a minute!" Rip interjected. "Let's think this out before we go blowing off. If they want ties at Chipeta, then there's nothing to Curry's story that we're going to be shut out of White River Junction. That's the first thing that hits me. If we're going to accept their freight, what difference does it make whether we haul their ties or ours?"

Jeannie said, "It'll make a considerable difference, Rainbow. They're offering us the same price at Chipeta that we'd get from the Midland. There's some profit in that, to say nothing of the fact that shipping three to four cars a week to White River Junction will tie up our limited equipment. I've sat here for an hour, thinking it over. At first, I felt as Grumpy does. But frankly, I've changed my mind; I can't see how it will hurt us. We can't keep them from getting ties. If we won't supply them, someone else will."

"All right, have it yore way!" the little one grumbled,

though he was far from convinced of the wisdom of it. "More knucklin' under, I call it! Con around?"

"He's over in the roundhouse, working on Number 3," Jeannie answered. "He's got a man helping him put in the new flues."

"We better walk over, Rip, and tell him to git word to Flynn."

Rainbow saw that Jeannie didn't understand. He told her what Bent had had to say.

"I think Jim should be told to be on guard," she agreed. "How much longer is Bent going to stay on the mountain?"

"A day or two. There's no need to worry about him, Jeannie. At the first sign of anything suspicious down there, he'll pull out for Lively at once."

He and Grumpy were talking to Hanrahan, when they heard the up train blowing for Lively. The three of them walked back to the depot together. Rainbow was interested in hearing what Pop Burke, the conductor, might have to say. While waiting for Pop to come into the office, he glanced at the evening papers. The Denver and Pacific cut-off was still on the front pages, but the news was concerned with such things as a new bond issue and the letting of the contract for the completion of the Spanish Peak tunnel. An item of a few lines said that Lon Morgan and Mike Tovey had been returned to Wyoming.

Pop had news of a more important nature. He hadn't been flagged at Chipeta but he had deposited four men there, who, judging by the equipment they carried, were surveyors.

"We also had some express," he said. "Grub, I take it. When those fellows climbed aboard at the Junction, they didn't have any tickets; they paid the cash fare to Chipeta, and they didn't even ask if I'd let them off there. The D. and P. had cut into our wire, for sure, and taken off your message to me, Jeannie."

"They could do it easily enough," she asserted. "I've suspected it was being done on several occasions, in the past."

The partners knew what the Thunder River and Northern's set-up was in White River Junction. It maintained its own agent-operator there, but it shared the depot with the Midland and Denver and Pacific.

"It wouldn't be necessary for them to cut in on our wire," she continued. "Any experienced operator, hearing a receiver tapping, could take off what it's saying. Maybe we better start sending in code, Pop. I'll work out something."

Bent had seen the new arrivals get down from the up train. Knowing the crew would report the incident on reaching Lively, he decided to remain where he was.

When morning came, the surveyors began running levels with their transits. Otherwise the day proved to be long and tedious. Shag Kissick and his men were not in Chipeta just to play cards and sun themselves, however. That evening, after nightfall, he and two of his gang opened the Y into the mainline and proceeded up the tie spur.

"They'll have two cars loaded by now," Shag told his cohorts. "All we gotta do is start 'em rollin' and they'll go tearin' hell-bent down the canyon."

They reached the vicinity of the camp and found it still awake. An hour passed before Shag gave the word to close in. In addition to setting the brakes, Flynn had placed wooden chocks under the wheels of the first car. With the aid of crowbars, Shag and his men removed the chocks. After that, it was only a half minute's work to release the brakes. A little pushing did the rest. The cars began to roll. The grinding wheels aroused the camp. Too late big Jim realized what had happened. Faster and faster the loaded cars sped down the siding in the moonlight. He let out an enraged roar.

"The dirty scuts!" he bawled. "They pried out the chocks and sint thim cars down the grade!"

Nothing was to be seen of Shag and his men. That was hardly necessary; Jim knew where to place the blame. In his way, he was a man of action. Pausing only to pull on his boots and his britches he started across the hills at a dog trot for Lively.

The runaway cars continued to gather speed. Presently, they were traveling at forty miles an hour, threatening to leave the uncertain rails at every curve. The heavy ties were flying right and left, sailing through the air as though they were toothpicks.

Faster and faster they went, the wheel flanges screaming. Somehow, they hit the Y without piling up and shot down the canyon. They were doing sixty now. The first sharp curve in the trough Thunder River had cut between the sheer walls of Ute Canyon spelled disaster. The forward car left the rails. The one behind bucked into it and both went shooting into the air and crashed into the opposite rocky wall with a splintering thunder that could have been heard for miles.

Up on Moran Mountain, Bent heard it. He mistook it for an explosion as he listened to the reverberation rolling across the far corridors of the Thunder River Range.

He was helped to his conclusion by the absence of any sign of excitement down below, in Chipeta. Throwing his saddle on his pony, he raced down the trail with a reckless regard for his safety.

Lively was sound asleep when he dashed up to the hotel. Running up the stairs, he hammered on the partners' door. Rainbow flung it open.

"Get dressed!" Bent burst out excitedly. "There's hell to pay down in the canyon! Sounded like an explosion!"

The tall man tried to take it calmly. "Get Con and Junie, Bent. Tell them to get Number 2 ready to roll. Grump and I will meet you at the depot in ten minutes."

Grumpy had piled out of bed. He was a grotesque figure as he stood there in his underwear, blinking owlishly. Bent was already rushing down the stairs.

"Explosion, he says!" the little one jerked out. "What do you figger it means?"

"I don't know!" Rip snapped. "Don't stand there jabbering! Get dressed—and strap your guns on! Whatever this is, tain't going to be pleasant!"

CHAPTER 13

BEFORE THE Hanrahans were routed out of bed and had Number 2 ready to roll, forty minutes passed. Con was of the opinion that Bent's "explosion" would prove to have been a snowslide.

"A bad wan sounds like thunder," he told Rip. "Shure and I hope it was only dynamite. The worst that could do would be to wreck a few feet of track; a bad snowslide might tie us up for weeks."

Bent had climbed aboard the tender. The partners were about to follow, when Jim Flynn, badly winded, came panting up the track, waving his arms excitedly.

That he was in Lively at all, and especially at this time of night, told the partners at once that, whatever the trouble, it was related to the tie camp. Forewarned, they listened, faces set, as the foreman blurted out his story.

"I told you it was no explosion!" Con growled. "It's worse! I know what we'll find!"

"We won't rush off half-cocked," Rainbow declared. "We'll need rails and tools. You know what will be required, Con.

We'll load everything on a flatcar. You take charge. If we work all night, it may not be necessary to cancel the morning train."

"We'll need men, Rip," said Hanrahan.

"We'll get them at the tie camp. If Flynn's boys can use an adz, they can swing a sledge."

It was after eleven when they steamed out of Lively. At Chipeta, they took the Y and ran up to the tie camp. The big storm lantern, mounted on the engine's smokebox, cut a bright swath along the rails. Con groaned as he saw the ties that had been flung right and left from the runaway cars.

They found the tie camp awake. With Flynn's crew perched on the flatcar, Con backed down to the Y and headed into Ute Canyon. Running slowly, and leaning out the cab window, eyes glued on the rails, he slapped on the air as the storm lantern revealed the twisted rails and torn up roadbed, where the cars had plunged into the river. The cars, themselves, had been reduced to kindling wood. The swift-flowing river was still carrying away the debris.

The partners and the others got down and looked things over.

"It ain't so bad," said Con. "With a little sweat, we'll have things opened up by daylight . . . Jim, you and your boys start clearing away. Toss everyt'ing into the river."

Hoping to set an example, the partners toiled with the rest. It was an eerie business, working by the light from the engine, the din of the roaring river filling their ears and the inhospitable walls of the canyon rising for several thousand feet, on either hand.

"This will cost us a couple thousand dollars," Grumpy ground out, during a brief respite. "Are we goin' to let 'em git away with it—do nothin'?"

"Not if I know it." Rainbow's face was hard and flat as he spoke. "They've asked for it and we'll show them we can dish it out, too."

Dawn was breaking before the new rails were brought up and spiked down. When daylight chased the shadows out of the canyon, Rainbow gritted his teeth as he saw how complete was the destruction of the cars and how few of the ties remained to be salvaged. Jim Flynn was at his side and read his thought.

"It won't pay to pick thim up, boss. And we broke our backs cutting thim. We wanted to make a good showing for you and Jeannie."

"Jim—you told me the other day that if I could promise your boys a good fight, they'd come running. Does that still go?"

"Does it! You say the wurrd and we'll run that gang out of Chipeta!"

"Your men are tired, Jim."

"This morning breeze will freshen thim up. Let 'em rest a few minutes. They'll lick their weight in wildcats!"

"All right, pass the word to them," said Rainbow. "Tell them to slip the handles out of their picks while they're resting."

"Shure, I don't need no pickhandle!" big Jim averred. "Me fists are good enough for me, and I'll take care of Shag Kissick, meself!"

The men shouted their approval when they learned what was ahead of them. Even Con tightened his belt and was anxious to be off.

"Suppose you stay with the engine when we pull into Chipeta," Rip told him. "We know which cabins they're in. They will be waiting for us; they certainly heard us go down the canyon last night. On the other hand, if we catch them asleep and surround them, we'll pile into them as they come running out. It'll make it easier, Con."

"And what would you have me do?"

"Give us five minutes to get set, then start blowing the whistle."

"Very well," Con muttered, not liking the arrangement at all. "Junie, you'll stay in the cab with me."

"After what they did to us?" Young Hanrahan demanded incredulously. "Not a chance! The next thing they'll be doing will be to loosen a rail and Dennis and me will be pitched into the river like them flats was!"

"I'll stay with Con," Grumpy volunteered. "We won't take no chance on them stealin' the engine."

The train backed into Chipeta. The men were quiet enough, but old Number 2 couldn't turn a wheel without clanking and retching. That Shag and his gang could be unaware of what impended, seemed a forlorn hope. However, Rainbow held to his plan. The two cabins were surrounded and Con began using the whistle cord. No one ran out into their arms.

Rainbow turned to Bent and Flynn. "Come on!" he told them. "We'll bust in here and see what goes!"

The door was unlocked. They slammed it back and rushed in. The cabin was empty. Shag had kept his men awake all night, expecting there would be reprisals. They were hidden now in a building across the way that had once housed Chipeta's noisiest saloon. Though he saw that he was outnumbered, he didn't propose to be caught there, like rats in a trap. Making the most of a surprise attack, he and his men rushed out of the old saloon, swinging their clubs, and took the enemy in the rear.

It gave them a momentary advantage, but Flynn and his Irishmen weathered the attack and began swinging their pick-handles with a vengeance. On both sides, men went down, faces bloody, got up and were felled again.

The two surveyors and their rodmen had not felt called on to join forces with Kissick. To be sure that their instruments would not be wrecked, they had retired from Chipeta and scrambled up the mountain.

Shag darted at Rainbow. Jim Flynn tripped him neatly and kicked the club out of the giant's hands. "Come on," Jim taunted, using his boot to give emphasis to his demand, "git to your feet and let's see you use thim fists!"

The two of them slugged it out, toe to toe for several minutes. For all of his prowess, the foreman was getting the worst of it. Shag flung a long, whistling right at him. His ham-like fist caught Flynn on the jaw, lifted him to his toes and turned his legs to rubber. Down he went, but Junie Hanrahan was there to take his place.

Shag had a bad cut under his right eye. Junie opened it

wider and moved around him, rocking the big fellow with rights and lefts. He couldn't drop him, however. Bent Curry pitched in. Kissick seemed invulnerable, and between them, they could not drive him to his knees.

Rainbow had little time for that. A hairy, broad-chested bully had him pinned up against a cabin wall. The best he could do was to keep the man off balance with one short, sharp left jab after another. They were punishing blows, but they seemed to have as little effect as rain. Suddenly, his adversary backed away a step and then came in with arms wide, obviously intent on wrestling him to the ground. Rip brought his right knee up and planted it in the man's stomach. It drove the air out of the latter with a loud wh-o-osh.

Knowing he had the other helpless for a moment, Rip brought a right hand up from his knees. All the drive he could muster was behind it. A foolish look spread over the rough's face and he crumpled up like the proverbial empty grain sack.

Busy as he was, Shag had an eye for what was going on around him. Though he was doing all right, personally, he was experienced enough to know that this Donnybrook was going against him. He had lost such fights before, and survived. It explained why the Denver and Pacific found him so valuable. He was a firm believer in the old adage that he who fights and runs away, lives to fight another day. He was ready to run now. He had no sense of loyalty to his men to hold him back; he could pick up a hundred others who would do his bidding just as readily. All that was needed was good wages, and his thugs were always well paid.

Con was leaning so far out of the cab as he watched the melee that he was in danger of pitching out on his face. Shag saw him, but he failed to notice Grumpy, who was flattened out on the tender. To bowl a man or two aside and make a dash for the engine, less than a hundred yards away, seemed well within the possibilities. He knew how to operate a locomotive. Once he was in the cab, he'd toss Con out, put on the steam and make off down the canyon for White River Junction. He had done what he had been expected to do at Chipeta; destroy T. R. and N. property, cost the new owners several thousand dollars and give them a taste of what they could expect if they didn't come to terms. A lost fight and a few broken heads would be written off as of no account, by D. and P. officials.

As he girded himself for his move, the unmistakable smell of wood smoke reached his nostrils. It came from somewhere behind him. He didn't dare to turn his head; Bent and Junie Hanrahan were boring in on him. It was only a moment or two before he heard the crackling of flames.

"Fire!" one of Jim Flynn's men yelled. "Look at the roof, over there!"

A patch of flame a foot square one moment, and then the entire roof was ablaze. The wind was stiff enough to carry the sparks to the next cabin. In seconds, it too was burning.

Shag waited no longer; he knew this was his opportunity. Bolting into Bent, he knocked him aside and raced for the engine. He was within a few yards of the tracks, when Grumpy set his gun to bucking. Those spattering shots, all deliberately high, stopped Shag. Instead of turning back, he swung off to the south, determined to go down the canyon on foot. A slug kicked up the dust in front of him. A second cried an even sterner warning.

It turned Shag back. He found Rainbow confronting him, gun in hand.

"Line up alongside the engine with the rest of your gang!" the tall man ordered.

The fire was making such rapid headway that all hands were being forced down to the tracks. The heat was now so great that cabin after cabin sprang into flame with an explosive report. That not a stick would be left standing in Chipeta, including the depot, was obvious.

"We better git out of here, Rip!" Grumpy called down from the tender. "What you goin' to do with these birds?"

"Send them down the canyon."

"Git 'em aboard the flatcar and we'll start rollin'!"

"No, they're going to hoof it," the tall man corrected. "You get down here with me; the two of us will ride the pilot. Con, you keep the engine moving just fast enough for them to keep ahead of you. Grump and I will see that no one turns back."

He thanked Flynn and his tie-cutters for all they had done and told them to return to camp.

Sparks were igniting the roof of the little depot by the time the partners had Kissick and his roughs moving down the tracks. With a warning toot, Con put on the steam and the wheels began to turn. Bent, riding the tender, looked back to see Chipeta all aflame.

Shag's crew were a battered, sorry-looking bunch, as they were herded down Ute Canyon. In addition to their hurts, they had lost what few personal belongings they owned. Dull-witted they might be, but they knew Shag had tried to run out on them. Left to themselves, they would have ganged up on him and pitched him into the river and cheered as they watched him drown.

Shag glanced back over his shoulder repeatedly at the partners. It had begun to dawn on him that they were not to be held lightly. He eyed the river with an obscure interest, weighing his chances of diving into it and making his way across to the canyon wall. Risky as it would have been, he would have attempted it if he had found a place where he could crawl out and make good his escape. Melting snows in the high places had turned Thunder River into a foaming torrent, the white water licking the sheer granite wall with a sinister swish. He could see no place where he could hope to find a toe-hold.

Con kept Number 2 clanking along until he ran out of the canyon. Rip signalled him to stop. Getting down from the pilot, he walked up to Kissick.

"We part company here, Shag," he said thinly. "You cut across country for the Junction. Keep off this roadbed. If we catch you on it, we'll shoot and ask questions later. You understand that?"

"What the hell!" Kissick sneered. "You ain't scaring me! I'll be back!"

"Sure you will. But not today . . . Get going!"

The tall man stood there until he lost sight of them. Grump

and he got up in the cab and Con backed into Chipeta again. All that was left of the ghost camp was a smouldering ruin. Debris from the burned depot littered the track. It had to be cleared before the return run to Lively could be made. After taking the Y, Con examined the scorched ties, making sure they had not been damaged enough to be dangerous.

"We can be moving," he said, after using a sledge on some loosened spikes. "It's 6:45. It'll give you time to have breakfast before you pull out for the Junction, Junie."

"You up to it, Junie?" Rip inquired. "You've had a hard night. That cut on your chin should be fixed up."

"Just a scratch," young Hanrahan declared. "It won't stop me from firing this old boiler." He added laughingly, "We gave them hell, didn't we?"

"It's too soon to do any cheering," said Rainbow. "It'll be dog eat dog, from now on. Just to be on the safe side, Grump and I will ride down to the Junction and back with you today. There may be trouble at the other end."

"I reckon there'll be trouble at our end," the little one declared grimly. "Bent's old man knows by now that Chipeta's gone up in smoke. The least he'll do will be to slap a lawsuit on us."

Rip thought that altogether unlikely. He explained why. "We've got Curry on record as saying that Shag and his gang were in Chipcta with his permission, protecting his property. That makes them his agents and he's responsible under law for what they do. He'll swear it wasn't at his direction that our cars were sent down the grade and piled up in the canyon. That won't put him in the clear—unless he'll come through with the information that the Denver and Pacific are paying Shag's wages. That's the last thing in the world he'd do."

"Good grief! Don't tell me yo're goin to try to collect damages for them cars and ties!" Grumpy got out incredulously. "No question but Kissick did the job, but we can't prove it!"

"Of course we can't," Rainbow agreed. "Curry can't prove we burned out Chipeta. You leave him to me, Grump. If he starts ranting, I'll cool him off."

CHAPTER 14

THE MAIDEN aunt, with whom Jeannie lived, had awakened her as soon as the news swept over Lively that Chipeta was burning. She was still dressing, when Link Easter rapped on the front door. Drifting smoke from the burning camp now hung over town, but it wasn't only news of the fire that Link brought; he had discovered that the partners and the Hanrahans had left town on Number 2 during the night.

"Bent was here, they tell me at the hotel," he ran on. "I reckon he went with them. That was hours ago, Jeannie. Have you any idea what's behind all this?"

She protested her complete ignorance. She was wide awake by now.

"Whatever the cause, it came unexpectedly; I'm sure of that," she said, trying to pull herself together. "There's been a fight with Shag Kissick's crowd, but I don't believe the boys took the engine and ran down there for that."

Old Link nodded soberly. "I agree with you. I don't give a dang about the fire; Chipeta was bound to go up in smoke, sooner or later. Mark Curry will think otherwise, but his rantin' won't bother me. I want to know what's happened to Rip and the boys. I'll round up some men and git down there. It won't do no good to tell you not to worry. Jest don't go to pieces, Jeannie. Rip and the little fella know their way around; they ain't likely to git over their heads . . . I'll see you at the depot before I pull out."

Though Jeannie finished dressing quickly and left the house a few minutes later, she found a crowd gathering, when she reached the office. Without exception, they were townspeople, all sympathetic to her cause, but there was nothing she could tell them.

On reaching her desk, she looked for a note, thinking Rainbow might have left some word for her. There was nothing, however, and as she settled down to the agony of waiting for definite news of what had happened, she saw Marcus Curry stamp past the window. He pushed through the office door a moment later, his round jowly face lined with rage.

"You and your friends will pay for this!" he thundered. "I'll show you people whether there's some law in this country or not!"

Link was right behind him and heard it.

"What do you mean, bustin' in here and threatenin' Jeannie that way?" he demanded fiercely. "Why don't you wait till you know what yo're talkin' about before you go to blowin' off? There was a time when folks started runnin' for the cyclone cellar whenever you began barkin', but that don't go no more. Jest suppose you clear out of here now and leave this girl alone."

"Why, you old lop-eared fossil, don't you dare to lay a hand on me!" Curry roared, as the sheriff grabbed him by the arm.

"Git!" Link whipped out. There was something in his slitted eyes that carried conviction, and the banker did not stand on the order of his going. The old man slammed the door and turned the key. "You keep it locked," he told Jeannie. "If Mark's got any blowin' off to do, let him do his talkin' to Rip and Grumpy."

"You shouldn't have made an issue of it, Link. He won't forgive you. After all, he's always helped to elect you."

"Yeh, and loaded on my shoulders the job of policin' this town as well as the county, to save the eight hundred a year we used to pay a town marshal! Any support he'd be wouldn't elect me dog catcher now—not after what he's done . . . You got the wire open to the Junction?"

"It's open, but there's no news," Jeannie replied. "Get back as quickly as you can, Link. I'll be counting the minutes until I know . . . Listen! That's Number 2 coming now!"

The sheriff hurried to the window. "It's her!" he agreed. "Jeannie—you stay inside; I'll git the boys in here, pronto. Y'understand?"

She nodded. Through the window, she saw Bent leap to the platform before the train stopped moving. He brushed past his father without a glance and ran into the office and took her in his arms.

"Your clothes are torn, Bent!" she cried. "Your right eye is almost closed!"

"Yeh, I look pretty tough, I reckon," he answered, with a grin. "You should have seen the guy that gave me that shiner."

Breathless, she listened as he poured out his tale of what had occurred during the night and that morning. Even more graphic was the account the partners gave Link.

Mark Curry heard every word of it, as Rip and Grumpy intended he should. The tall man whirled on him without warning.

"Of course, you didn't know anything about this, Curry," he rapped, with withering sarcasm. "It never crossed your mind that the innocent little bunch of blacklegs you had in Chipeta were there for any other purpose than to guard those rotten old buildings."

"I knew nothing about it!" Curry shot back.

"Well, you know about it now. They got their orders from someone. If not from you, who was it? The Denver and Pacific?"

Marcus Curry squared his shoulders and let out a venomous

blast. "You do your talking now, I'll do mine when I get you men in front of a jury!"

"Piffle! Bluff!" Grumpy snorted contemptuously. "You ain't sayin' nothin' now and you won't say nothin' later! You know you'll incriminate yore crowd if you do!"

"What about the fire, Rip?" Link interjected. "Did you fellas set it?"

"We did not. Kissick had a fire going in the cabin where they did their cooking. One of his men upset the stove by accident. We've got all the witnesses we need. If you've got anything further to say to us, you'll have to say it across the breakfast table; Number 2 is departing on schedule this morning, and we're riding her. As for you, Mr. Curry, you can do your talkin in court, if and when you get around to it."

The crowd opened to let Grumpy and him through and then turned to enjoy Curry's discomfiture. Men joined in the laughter at his expense who would not have dared such an affront a week or two ago.

Though the partners had but a few minutes at their disposal, they stopped for a word with Jeannie. She was as angry as her red hair gave her a right to be.

"Bent's told me what they did to us," she got out excitedly. "Cars wrecked! Roadbed torn up! It makes my blood boil!"

"It isn't the end of the world," said Rip. "They'll surely hand us worse than that before this scrap is over."

"I suppose they will," she agreed wearily. "But dammit, it needn't have happened! We might have guessed that they would try to send those cars down the grade!"

The tall man had to smile at her vehemence. "You *are* mad, aren't you?"

"I'm so mad I'd like to punch Shag Kissick's nose! I know it's foolish to get worked up about it, but I've been sitting here taking it on the chin so long that something had to give."

Grumpy put an arm around her and gave her a fatherly hug. "You stick to yore knittin', Jeannie. They won't pull that trick on us a second time; Jim Flynn's got orders to chain the cars to the tracks till we're ready to move 'em."

"That's locking the barn after the horse is gone, Grumpy."

"Mebbe so," he acknowledged. "But if the barn's still there, it's worth savin'." He gave her arm an affectionate pat. "I figger we collected a little interest on the account this mornin', in runnin' 'em out of Chipeta. And I reckon they'll hear from us again. When things git tough, Jeannie, you got to git tough with 'em."

The partners made the round trip to the Junction that day and the next without encountering any hint of reprisal. Coming up on the second afternoon, they ran into rain below Ute Canyon. They thought nothing of it at the time, but it was the beginning of a late spring storm that was to drive down unremittingly for the rest of the week, sending every creek and rivulet over its banks. The last traces of snow disappeared in Mears Pass. Down in Ute Canyon, the Thunder River and Northern tracks were soon under water in several places. Trains had to be cancelled.

Rainbow went down with Grumpy and Con and looked the situation over. Dead trees, brush, everything the river could tear loose, was being carried down from above. The wrecked flatcars were barrier enough to catch most of it, and it was jamming there, with the water building up behind it.

"Dynamite is the answer," Con asserted. "We'll be in real trouble unless we blow up that stuff."

They worked all afternoon at it, scrambling over the dripping, treacherous wall. Water shot into the air for a hundred feet when the heavy charge was exploded. The released flood waters tore down the canyon with a deafening roar. Stretches of track began to reappear.

"The roadbed could be built up and this sort of trouble avoided," said Rip.

"Shure it could," Con agreed. "It wouldn't cost much. But whin yo're strapped for money, anything is expensive. We'll have some track washed out. That won't tie us up more than a day or two, once we can get at it."

The rain passed and the river fell rapidly. Hanranhan recruited a work force from Flynn's tie-cutters and went to work clearing the roadbed and replacing a number of twisted rails. Forty-eight hours later the first train in four days went through to the Junction.

That evening, Grumpy summed up the situation in a few words, when he said, "Looks like we got a bear by the tail and can't let go. Our money's goin' out a lot faster than it's comin' in."

"That's a fact," Rainbow agreed. "But its no more than I expected. We may have to put every dollar we own on the line before we're through. That was the gamble we took; we can't pull out now."

"Hellsfire, who's sayin' we should?" the little one snapped. "I jest figger we oughta git a little break, now and then."

They got one, a few days later. A cattle buyer appeared in Lively and bought the Painted Meadows calf crop. Five carloads of the little fellows were shipped out. The brief hum of activity had a tonic effect on Jeannie. It was over all too soon.

"It would take so little for the T. R. and N. to justify its existence," she told Rip and Grumpy.

"It was a nice little shot in the arm," the tall man replied. "Flynn's boys are pilin' up the ties. No confirmation yet on the deal with the Denver and Pacific, eh?"

"I haven't heard a word since I asked for a contract."

"Don't do anythin' till you git it," Grumpy advised. "It ain't likely you will hear till they put a gang of men into Chipeta to unload the stuff. Pop Burke tells me a D. and P. construction train rolled into the White River Junction yesterday afternoon. It may mean somethin'."

Bent came in as they sat there. He had been over in the roundhouse helping Con. "He's firing Number 3," he announced. "Going to run her out for a little trial. She really looks good—painted and polished up. The old boy is proud of the job he's done. I'm going to ride in the cab with him and give him a hand. He's going to run down to the Chipeta Y and back. You fellows want to come along?"

"We shore do," Grumpy declared. "We'll walk over with you now."

Con backed Number 3 out of the roundhouse proudly and pulled up at the depot. Jeannie ran out to congratulate him.

"She looks fine, Con!"

"That she does, if you don't mind my saying so," Con replied, with a broad grin. "And she's perking as pretty as you please."

With a toot of the whistle, he rolled out of Lively and chuffed away to the south. He was beaming when he steamed into Chipeta, twenty minutes later.

"She's tight as a drum," he declared. "I believe she could do t'irty-five if I opened her up. She goes on the run to the Junction in the morning."

They found Chipeta as it had been for days, blackened, deserted. Well up on the northern flank of Moran Mountain, they could see the white speck that was the tent the surveyors had erected after leaving the old camp.

"Must be workin' toward the Pass," Grumpy said speculatively.

"I imagine they are," Rip agreed. "The first chance we get, we're going over Mears Pass and see what, if anything, the Denver and Pacific is doing in Middle Park. It'll take us a couple days, but we ought to know."

On returning to Lively, Jeannie greeted them with the news that she had just received a request by wire that freight cars be spotted into the Junction the following day. She had also been informed that the contract covering the purchase of the ties was in the mail.

"It means they're movin' into Chipeta," Grumpy observed. "If they need cars, they're bringin' in equipment and a work crew."

"I hope that's what it means," was Rainbow's sober comment. "Did they say how many cars they wanted?"

"No, but I imagine they know how few we have left," said Jeannie. "We have two on the siding at the Junction now, and four here. How will you handle it, Con?"

"I'll have to change my plans and put Number 3 on the heavy hauling; Number 2 ain't up to it. I'll need a fireman.

I can git Barney Doolin. He'll be all right, once I git some of the beer sweated outa him."

It took the Denver and Pacific four days to move into Chipeta. The little freight cars of the Thunder River and Northern, a scant forty feet in length, made little impression on the mountain of equipment that the big road poured into White River Junction. Mules, horses, scrapers, rails, a complete commissary, tents and men—upwards of a hundred—were set down at Chipeta.

One of the men was Shag Kissick, making good his boast that he would be back. he had a new gang of thugs with him—ten in all, according to the partners' estimate—and they were made of sterner stuff than the pickhandle-wielding bunch that had been run out. One look at them was enough for Grumpy.

"Hired gunmen," he asserted. "You could spot 'em with one eye shut!"

"Texans by their look," said Rainbow. "The offscourings of the Panhandle cow towns. You wondered what the riding stock was for. You know now; those gents are going to fork the broncs and do some scouting, evidently."

The partners had been on Number 3 with Con every day, keeping a close eye on what was coming in. The construction boss and his foremen were easily identifiable. Experienced men, they took charge of the unloading and under their direction a tent city sprang up along the river in a few hours.

During the afternoon of the fourth day, the last carload of material was hauled up Ute Canyon and promptly unloaded. Everything had been handled with efficiency and dispatch. The partners expected the work to begin at once. But twenty-four hours passed, and not a spadeful of earth was turned.

The contract for the ties had arrived. Flynn had two carloads ready for delivery. Rip and Grumpy saw them put on the Chipeta siding. The inactivity there puzzled the little man.

"What are they waitin' for, Con? They got everythin'."

Rainbow had his own answer, but he was interested in hearing what Con Hanrahan had to say.

"They're waiting for the head man to arrive," said Con.

"This is a big operation, and in enemy territory, so to speak. Steve Lundy is a good construction boss; he can handle that end of it; Shag and his gunmen can take care of the dirty work; but the D. and P. will send someone up to throw his weight around. Somebody like Sam Dunlap or little Ambrose MacDonald."

"You're right; no question about it," Rip commented. "Whoever it is, he'll have authority to call the turn without running down to the Junction to get his orders."

The correctness of Con's surmise was borne out the following afternoon, when the up train brought Ambrose MacDonald, a small staff of clerks and a group of surveyors and engineers up the canyon. Macdonald, now in his middle fifties, had been a wheel horse for the Denver and Pacific for years. He was a quiet, affable man, by choice, and utterly ruthless where the interests of the D. and P. were concerned. It had often been said of him that, figuratively speaking, he made the snowballs that others threw. It explained why his name seldom appeared in the headlines. Had he been able to arrange it, he would have effaced himself completely and let the results of his labors in the company's behalf speak for themselves.

The construction camp sprang to life with Ambrose MacDonald's coming. The surveyors who had been up on Moran Mountain for days, came down and joined the others. Stakes were driven; the grading crew went to work; drillers tackled intervening ledges of solid rock that had to be blasted out of the way. All through the noon hour the charges were exploded, some of them so heavy that they could be heard as far away as Lively.

During the afternoon, a number of the curious rode down from town to watch the work. Rainbow and Grumpy observed it from a distance.

"On their way to Mears Pass," the little one muttered glumly. "They ain't foolin', Rip!"

"Maybe they mean it; maybe it's just a grand bluff to convince us that they don't need the Thunder River and Northern. They could spend a hundred thousand dollars here and

it would be a cheap price to pay if it whipped us into line."
Rip's mouth had a determined set. "They'll find they're wasting their time; they can build over Mears Pass, or over Pikes
Peak, but they won't go down Ute Canyon . . . If you've seen
enough, lets head back to town."

They had jogged along for a mile or more, when Grumpy
said, "I ain't seen anythin' in the papers about them bein'
granted a right of way across the Thunder River Range. But
I reckon they could wangle it through the Legislature without
any noise bein' made about it."

"You can be sure they took care of that," the tall man
declared. "And you can be sure that Lively realizes by now
that it's going to be by-passed if the Denver and Pacific can
get away with it."

They found Jeannie going over the freight bills for the last
few days.

"It'll give the road the best month it's had in years," she
said without enthusiasm. "I could get excited about it if it
were a windfall. But I know it isn't. I keep thinking of what
you said, Grumpy—that they're helping us to dig our own
grave."

"That doesn't sound like fighting talk to me," Rainbow
objected, his tone sharper than he realized. "It may be their
grave they're digging. Suppose we wait and see."

Ambrose MacDonald appeared in Lively the next day and
arranged with various merchants for supplies to be sent down
to the camp. The partners got the news from Bent. They
dropped into Louie Bannerman's store and spoke to him about
it.

"It's a slick trick, throwing a little business our way," Louie
told them. "But it ain't fooling nobody. I was going to put
it up to you. A dollar is a dollar, as the saying goes, but I
don't want to do anything to weaken your hand."

"You take all you can get, Louie," Rip advised. "If they
didn't buy their supplies in Lively, they'd get them in White
River Junction."

Bannerman nodded. "I guess that's the way to look at it.
Some folks didn't believe you when you said the town was

going to be left behind. They believe you now. Thank God, we got you boys fighting for us . . . Do you really think you can stand up to them, Rip?"

"I do," Rainbow said simply. "Sooner or later, they'll have to do business with us."

CHAPTER 15

DESIROUS AS Rip was of going over Mears Pass and scouting what the Denver and Pacific was doing in Middle Park, he remained in Lively in the hope that Ambrose MacDonald would come to Grumpy and him with another offer. As a consequence, he spent hours on end in Jeannie's office at the depot. If he stepped out for only a few minutes, he was careful to tell her where he could be found.

The week-end went by uneventfully, however. He passed off MacDonald's failure to put in an appearance as of no consequence. Secretly, he was sorely disappointed. The little one and Jeannie pretended to feel as he did about it. They didn't fool Rainbow; he knew their confidence in ultimate victory was beginning to ebb.

The work at Chipeta was being pressed forward. It wasn't necessary for the tall man to observe it with his own eyes to be constantly aware of the progress being made. Every day, a score of townspeople rode down to watch the work for an hour or two. On returning to Lively, they reported what they had seen.

Bent Curry rode down on Tuesday afternoon, with instructions from the partners to find out what Shag and his hired gunslingers were doing. It was late in the evening before he returned. He found Rip and Grumpy seated downstairs at the hotel. He had little to tell them.

"They're just lolling around camp, not doing a lick of work. I was up on the mountain. I watched them with the binoculars till dark."

"It might not be a bad idea for you to keep an eye on them right along," said Rip. "If you see them heading down into the canyon, get word to us or Con as quickly as you can. Our trains are feeling their way through the gorge. Even so, one of them may hit a loosened rail and pitch off into the river. You know what that would do to us, Bent."

They spent half an hour together. Bent had been gone only a few minutes, when Jeannie ran in, her face white with excitement.

"Quick!" she gasped, grasping the back of a chair to steady herself. "I went down to the office to get some papers. I saw a light in the roundhouse. I knew Con was working tonight. I went over to speak to him. Through the window, I saw two men removing the drive rod from Number 3. I—I couldn't see anything of Con."

"Good grief!" Grumpy burst out furiously. "If they make off with the drive rod, that engine will be out of commission for a couple weeks while we're waitin' to git a new one!"

"Did they see you, Jeannie?" Rainbow demanded, his voice tense.

"I—I'm sure they didn't—"

"You find Link," he told her. "Tell him to get down in a hurry. We'll meet him there; it'll take us only a minute to get our guns."

It was Con's habit to close the two sets of wide, double doors of the roundhouse over night; it kept out the wind and cold on raw evenings, when he might be working on the engines, as well as discouraging the town's small fry from running over the place. The only way of fastening them was by putting a wooden bar through brackets on the inside. A small door, set in a wing of a larger one, permitted him to enter and leave at will. It too was innocent of a lock.

A series of grimy windows, panes of glass missing from many of them and the gaping holes boarded up, ran along the sides of the ramshackle building. Entrance could have been had through the windows, but the partners took it for granted that whoever was inside had passed through the little door. Quartering across the tracks, Grumpy caught the faint glow of a lantern within. They stopped for a moment and heard metal striking metal.

"The dirty skunks are still in there," the little one muttered. "We can chalk this up to Shag Kissick. Come on! You cover 'em from the window; I'll go through the door!"

"Stay where you are!" Rip whipped out. "Those birds are armed; they'll shoot it out at the drop of a hat."

"So what?" the little one demanded indignantly.

"We're waiting for Link. When we go in there, we're going in shooting. I want him to understand that. You talk about where we'd be if they made off with the drive rod. Where do you think we'd be if they crippled the other engine, too? We'd be left here high and dry. How would we get new ones in? By mule team?"

They saw Link coming. Jeannie had told him enough to put him in a lather.

"Did you hear that?" Grumpy growled as the ring of steel hitting the concrete floor rang out. "That was a drive rod!"

"To hell with the engines!" Link perked out. "They can be repaired! What about Con? God knows what they've done to him!"

"There's sure to be gunsmoke in this," said Rip. "How do you want to handle it?"

"You take a window, Grumpy," the sheriff ordered, without a moment's hesitation. "Find one with a glass out. Git 'em covered. Rip and me will go through the door. We'll bust in when we hear you yell out for 'em to hoist their hands. I'll give 'em a chance to surrender. If they won't play it that way, cut 'em down! I'll be responsible!"

Rainbow and he were at the door, waiting, when Grumpy

shoved his .45 through a gaping hole in a window and barked a peremptory summons for the two men to freeze where they were. Rip kicked the door open and leaped inside in time to see one of the pair use his boot on the lantern and send it rolling across the floor spurting oil. There was a second's blackness before the oil blazed up.

"They're in back of the tender!" Grumpy yelled from the window. In the garish, smoking light from the shattered lantern, he saw a gun barrel shoved out in that direction. He snapped a shot at it and it disappeared.

The shot boomed with a hollow sound in the closed roundhouse. Before its echo died away, Link darted around the engine and found himself in the semi-darkness between the two locomotives, which stood on parallel tracks. The man at whom Grumpy had fired leaped out from behind the tender and started to run around Number 2. Link could have dropped him, but he had his code and he called out for the man to throw up his hands. The latter, without breaking stride, escaped momentarily. The sheriff slapped a shot where the man had been, but he no longer had a target.

The second gunman had already swung around Number 2 and was moving up its far side, intent on reaching the door. When he got as far as the pilot, he saw Link and fired immediately.

The slug ploughed through the old man's right leg, but he didn't go down. Swinging around in the direction from which the shot had come, he saw his assailant, half-way to the door. He squeezed the trigger. Two shots rang out—his and one from Rainbow's gun. A bullet found its mark. From whose gun, there was no telling. Though staggered, the man reached the door only to come face to face with Grumpy, who had left the window and ran around the corner of the building to get into the fight.

For a split second, both men froze, badly startled. The little one was the first to snap out of it. Firing from the waist, he blasted the other out of the way.

"That's one of 'em!" he yelped. "Where's the other rat?"

"He's back of Number 2," Rip told him. "Link's been hit.

You take the right wall, Grump; I'll go down the other side. You stay where you are, Link. Drop him if you see him."

The cornered gunman retreated to the rear of the round-house. Picking up an empty nail keg, he hurled it through a window and attempted to scramble through after it only to find the window too high.

"All right!" he yelled. "I'm throwin' away my gun! I'm over here in the corner! Don't shoot!"

Grumpy was the first to reach him. "I got cha!" he rapped. "Keep on reachin' or I'll blow you apart!"

A strong smell of wood smoke had begun to pervade the rickety old building.

"It's the oil from that lantern!" Rainbow exclaimed. "You ride herd on this gent, Grump; I'll put the fire out before this shack goes up in flames!"

Finding a barrel of sand, he quenched the blaze without difficulty and lighted another lantern. Link hobbled around to him.

"Don't bother about me!" the old man snapped. "Find Con!"

Rip searched the roundhouse without success until he glanced into a little room where Hanrahan kept his tools. There, trussed up and gagged, lay Con. He had taken a terrible beating. Blood was still oozing down over his face from a gash in his scalp.

Outside, someone pounded on the door.

"Who is it?" Link cried.

"It's me, Bent!" was the answer. "Junie's with me!"

"Wal, git in here! Yo're needed!"

Between them, they quickly released Con. He was conscious, but it was a minute or two before he was able to speak.

"That damn rag they stuck in my mouth," he muttered apologetically, "it took my wind away."

"Take it easy," Rip told him. "We got both of them. One of them is going to make a job for the undertaker. Too bad it isn't Kissick."

"They're his boys, shure enough, Rip."

"No question about that. How did they get the jump on you, Con?"

"I was workin' on Number 2. I heard the door open. I didn't look up; I t'ought it was you or the little fella. The first t'ing I knew, they was on top of me. Wan of 'em hit me a belt on the head with a piece of pipe." He tried to smile. "That's whin the roof fell in, Rip. He was a tall gent, with a jaw a yard long and a nose to match."

"Grumpy, fetch that bird up here and let Con have a look at him!" Link growled.

"That's him. He's the gent!" Con declared, as Rip held up the lantern. "Shure and I'd like to let him have wan between the eyes!"

"Pop, I'll get a rig and take you to the doctor's," Junie spoke up. "Link's banged up, too."

"You'll git no rig, for me!" Con contradicted. "I'll walk outa here on me own legs, or I'll know why!"

"Shut up," Link told him. "Doc Trombly's got some work to do on both of us. You run up to the livery barn, Junie, and have Sweetman git down with a rig. And you dig Charlie Hughes outa bed and tell him I want him here pronto."

Bent had been looking for another lantern. He found half a dozen on a shelf. He lit one and walked over to where the dead man lay.

"I recognize this fellow, Rip," he called. "I saw him with Shag any number of times."

"Pick up his gun," Link told him. "And find this bird's hardware. Turn 'em over to Charlie, when he gits here."

The captured thug stared wooden-faced at the slain man. Though they were birds of a feather, their acquaintance had been brief. If there was an awareness in him of his own narrow escape from a similar fate, he gave no sign of it.

Rainbow joined Bent and they examined the damage done to the locomotives. The rod of Number 3 lay on the floor. A few minutes' work would replace it. The drive rod of the other engine had been removed, however, and they could find no trace of it.

Rip questioned the captured gunman but got nowhere.

"I won't tell yuh a thing," the lantern-jawed thug ground out for the third time.

"Bend a pickhandle over his head!" Con urged. "He'll talk, the dirty scut!"

"No," said Link, "I never beat up a prisoner yet, and I ain't beginnin' with this one. The rod's heavy; they can't have carried it very far."

The shooting had aroused the town. By the time Junie arrived with the liveryman, a sizable crowd had gathered at the roundhouse. Willing hands placed Link and Con in the carriage. Charlie Hughes, Link's deputy, took charge of the prisoner and led him off to jail. Rainbow called Junie aside.

"You can replace the rod on Number 3, can't you, Junie?"

"Certainly, with a little help. Not much of a job."

"We want her to roll out on schedule tomorrow morning," said Rip. "After you get through at the doctor's take your father home, then come back. Bent will give you a hand. In the meantime, we'll organize a search party and see if we can't find Number 2's shaft."

"What about that thing on the floor?" Grumpy queried, indicting the body. "We leavin' it there?"

"Charlie Hughes is sending the coroner down to take charge," Rip told him. "We'll wait a few minutes for him. You stick it out here, Bent. If we aren't back by the time Junie shows up, the two of you bolt the door before you go to work."

Chester Perry, the local undertaker, who served without pay as county coroner—an arrangement that was not without profit to him—arrived promptly and removed the body.

Little Hagedorn Creek, winding down the Painted Meadows on its way to join Thunder River, flowed along several hundred yards to the rear of the roundhouse. Rainbow led his search party in that direction, bobbing lanterns and improvised torches lighting up the night. Soon after they spread out along the creek, a cry was raised. The partners hurried that way and saw that the gunmen's broncs had been found. Grumpy seized a lantern and examined the surrounding brush. A broken twig, here and there, was enough to convince him that the two men had gone directly from the creek to the roundhouse.

"I miss my guess if they didn't lug that rod back here the same way," he told Rip. "I said we'd find it in the crick. I'm dead shore of it now."

The search concentrated on the creek in the immediate vicinity of the horses. It remained for a boy of eighteen to stumble upon the shaft, in mid-stream.

"By gum, we're in luck!" the little one exclaimed. "A couple of you young bucks wade in there and give the boy a hand!"

It was well after one o'clock before the damage to the locomotives had been repaired. The curious had long since drifted away.

"We ought to keep an armed guard on duty here," Bent suggested. "Shag may try this trick a second time. I'm willing to stick it out for the rest of the night."

"We'll have to hire someone," Rainbow agreed. "Putting locks on the doors wouldn't stop them. I'll ask Link to get us a reliable man. You stay here till daylight, Bent. We'll be down early."

Ike Sawtelle, the captured gunman, was brought into court next morning to face arraignment. Link was present, hobbling about on crutches. The slug that passed through his leg had not shattered any bones. Doc Trombly had advised him to keep off his feet for a week. It was a waste of breath on Doc's part.

The prosecutor asked that the prisoner be held on two charges: unlawful entry and assault on one count, and armed resistance against the person of the sheriff, on the other.

Sawtelle was quickly bound over to stand trial, with his bail fixed at ten thousand dollars.

"That'll hold him," Link said to the partners. "He ain't worth that much to the Denver and Pacific."

Link was mistaken. Ambrose MacDonald reached Lively before noon and conducted some business. In the course of it, he stopped at the bank. Half an hour later Marcus Curry appeared before the judge and posted bail for Sawtelle. The prisoner was brought up from jail and given his release. Before Lively knew what had happened, he had been hurried out of town.

When the news broke, it went winging from lip to lip and a wave of angry, violent protest rolled over Lively. Men gathered in little groups on the main street and threats were made, some veiled and some not so veiled, against Curry.

"Wal, I do be damned!" Grumpy exploded, when Rip hurried into the depot with word of what had happened. "Has the man gone crazy? He'll be lucky if he don't git a coat of tar and feathers for this!"

Young Bent joined them a moment later, looking haggard and outraged. "He must be mad! There's talk of stringing him up." He slumped into a chair and sat there shaking his head hopelessly. "I've tried—but I can't find an excuse for him." He glanced up at Rainbow suddenly. "You've been talking of going over the Pass into Middle Park. Promise me you won't go till this blows over, Rip. Whatever he is, he's my father; I've got to protect him."

"You do," the tall man said. "It does you credit to say so." The hint of a smile that so often hovered over his mouth had fled and his lean face had whipped hard and flat. "I'm no hand at turning the other cheek, but we won't leave town for two or three days . . . Have you talked with your father?"

"No—"

"Well, don't try to; it wouldn't do any good. Grumpy and I will stroll up the street and see if we can't laugh this thing off."

The little man shook his head. "How can you do it? You know Macdonald will run that gent outa the county by night-fall—that he'll never be back to stand trial."

"Of course I know it," Rainbow acknowledged. "That's my point. The ten thousand dollars that'll be forfeited will help to run this county for a year."

"And yo're goin' to purtend that that's okay with us?"

"We better, Grump; it's the only argument we've got."

CHAPTER 16

THE PARTNERS knew a dozen little ways in which to read temper of a town with some degree of accuracy. It was their experience that talk in itself, however wild and threatening, just as often proved to be an escape valve as a prelude to violence. There was talk in Lively, plenty of it.

"What do you think?" Grumpy asked, as Rip and he reached the courthouse. They had been stopped a dozen times and interrogated on their way up from the depot.

"I believe it's up to us," said Rainbow. "These people expected to find us breathing fire. It slowed them down some when they realized we were satisfied to see Curry get stuck for his ten thousand. Not that he is, Grump; that was Denver and Pacific money. Let's turn back. We'll drop into Bannerman's; a lot of this talk is starting there."

They saw Louie. He couldn't understand their attitude.

"Curry ought to have his horns clipped," he insisted. "Maybe it was D. and P. money. What difference does that make? He went to bat for that crowd and rubbed it in our nose. He knew Link had been shot up and hell banged out of Con."

"That's one way of lookin' at it," Grumpy admitted. "But you folks didn't git such a bad break out of it; we're rid of that crook, for one thing; the county's been saved the expense of a trial and there's ten thousand bucks in the kitty. That'll build some roads or help you to put an addition on the schoolhouse."

"That's my idea," Rip chimed in. "At ten thousand a head, I'd settle for every blackleg Kissick's got in camp."

They left Louie slightly bewildered. The situation remained tense for several hours but by early afternoon men, who had been of one opinion that morning, fell to arguing among themselves on the pros and cons of venting their wrath on Mark Curry. The partners began to breathe easier.

The bank closed at three. An hour later, Curry came out and walked home unattended. He was hooted at as he passed, but not a hand was laid on him.

"We can forget it for the present," said Rainbow. "But these folks will remember it, Grump. If there's another incident like this, Curry will be in trouble."

Several days passed. According to the Denver papers, work was proceeding beyond expectations in the tunnel under Spanish Peak, where improved power drills and modern machinery were being used. Of equal interest to the partners was the news that the Denver and Pacific was building up from Revelation. It removed any lingering doubt that it was in Ute Canyon that the showdown would come. More than ever Rainbow was anxious to see what was being done in Middle Park.

It was well into June already. Judging by the progress the Denver and Pacific was making at Chipeta, something would have to give before long. More freight was hauled up the canyon. One evening, a carload of laborers came up to augment Ambrose MacDonald's forces.

The ties that the T. R. and N. put on the siding seemed to melt almost as soon as they were delivered. Financially, the little road was in a better position than it had been in

Jeannie's memory. In spite of the tall man's optimism, she could not throw off the feeling that it was a false prosperity.

Con had lost only one day. Ten stitches had been taken in his scalp. He made light of it, as he did of his bruises and other cuts. Link, in the meantime, couldn't do much more than get down to his office. Con never lost an opportunity to drop in for some good-natured banter at the old man's expense.

"Shure and I never t'ought a little hole in your leg would put you on the shelf," Con twitted him one morning. "For years you been bragging that you was tougher than bullhide. If you'd been clipped on the head the way I was, it would have killed you."

"I reckon it would!" Link retorted irascibly. "There's somethin' inside my head. When Sawtelle went after you, he was hitting solid ivory. I'm surprised he didn't break an arm."

Bent came up with Con one afternoon. It was the first the partners had seen of him in three days. He had nothing to report. Shag and his gunslingers hadn't so much as taken a peek at Ute Canyon.

"MacDonald's surveying crew are getting pretty well up towards the Pass," Bent continued. "Shag sends a man or two up with them every day. You might think from that that he expects trouble up there."

"I hope he keeps on thinking so," said Rip. "You be ready to pull out with us tomorrow morning; we can't wait any longer to get over Mears Pass. We'll leave early and make it a point to be back in the afternoon of the third day. Things seem to have quieted down for a spell."

"As quiet as they're likely to be," Bent agreed. "We'll hit the high country in back of Dutch Altmeyer's. There's a trail up there that'll lead across to the Pass. We can go over without being seen. By the way, I was going to mention this and it slipped my mind. I don't know whether it means anything or not. This morning, I saw one of the cooks jerking the hide off a steer. I understood they were buying dressed beef, here in town."

"That's right," the little one assured him. "I've seen one

of the wagons bein' loaded most every mornin'. It's a big camp; takes a lot of meat to keep it goin'. Maybe they had to take a steer with the hair on it."

"I'll have to take that explanation with a grain of salt," Rainbow declared with cutting emphasis. "I haven't noticed that the butcher shops were short of beef . . . Did that cook slaughter the steer, Bent?"

"No, it was hanging when I happened to put the glasses on it. I haven't any reason for thinking so, but it struck me that Shag and his friends might be supplying the camp with rustled beef."

"That's the flash I got as soon as you mentioned it," said Rip. "That would be a profitable little game for them to work on the side."

"How long could they git away with it?" the little man demanded gruffly. "I'll put some stock in that when I hear Altmeyer or some other party bellerin' that they're losin' stuff."

Rainbow declined to argue the matter. Instead, he discussed the details of the trip. "We'll go as light as we can, just packing grub enough in our saddlebags to get us there and back. If you insist on a coffee pot, Grump, get hold of one and tie it on."

The breakfasted together and were across Altmeyer's Circle A spread and into the Thunder River foothills by midmorning. Before long, the going became steeper and they stopped several times to blow the ponies. Down below, the Painted Meadows unrolled before them. It was pleasant country, seen from their high perch. Grumpy gazed at it long and carefully.

"It shore takes the eye," he declared admiringly. "The grass is as green as I've ever seen it—virgin timber over there in the San Cristobals—all the mountain water a man could ever need. By grab," he sighed, "it's no wonder the Utes put up a fight when they saw themselves bein' euchred out of Painted Meadows!"

It was an old Ute trail that Bent was trying to find. Noon came before he located it.

"It'll take us right to the Pass," he said. "Uncle Joe Corbett used this trail when he moved the first cattle into the Meadows. If we're going to have a bite to eat, this is as good a place as any. You'll find that spring flowing ice-cold."

They nooned there for half an hour. The day was so peaceful, the air so invigorating with the tang of cedar and pine, that even this brief respite from the problems of the past few weeks was doubly welcome.

At Rip's request, Bent pointed out the course by which the old Indian trail reached Mears Pass. It appeared to be a thoroughly practicable route for a railroad to follow.

"The Utes had the run of this country for a hundred years, that we know of," said Bent. "They didn't stay cooped up in the Painted Meadows; their war parties found the easiest way into Middle Park. I don't believe any engineer can improve on it."

"Neither do I." The tall man turned and traced out the way they had come since leaving Lively. "It wouldn't add more than three miles to the distance between Denver and the west if the D. and P. came this way and swung down through town. The running time they'd save in dodging the curves and grades in getting down Moran Mountain would more than make up for it."

Grumpy put away his pipe and pushed his hat back on his head.

"That may be true," he declared, ready to argue the point, "but it's mileage they're tryin' to save, not money. The cut-off will cost them millions. They're floatin' bonds, boomin' their stock on the strength of the miles they're savin'. They won't add an inch to it, unless they're made to."

"That's the way I've seen this deal from the first," Rip responded. "They don't happen to hold all the cards, however; this cut-off is no cut-off at all unless they can grab Ute Canyon. So far, they haven't got it."

He refused to indulge in further argument. A few minutes later, they continued on their way. Unobserved, they went through the Pass and, still following the old trail, worked down out of the Thunder River Range. Bent pointed out

Spanish Peak, snow-capped the year around. It was forty miles away, but it seemed much nearer than that, an illusion common in these mountains.

"Are we goin' that far?" Grumpy queried. "I figgered you intended to find Priddy Crick. We was all purty much agreed, some time back, that the new road would come up that way."

"I haven't anything better to suggest," Rip replied. "By lining up Mears Pass and Spanish Peak, we know Priddy Creek is somewhere to the east of us. We'll keep on moving in that direction until we have to pull up for the night."

They saw no one for the rest of the day. Early next morning, however, they came on a prospector's cabin and found the owner at home. He was a bearded old-timer. Coming to the door, he looked them over suspiciously.

"Yo're strangers," he observed, his tone suggesting that he was not too pleased at seeing them. "Yuh lost?"

"You might say so," Grumpy answered, ready to do the talking for the three of them. The old prospector cackled scornfully.

"Yuh must be some of them railroad fellars that came over Berthoud, a few weeks back."

"That's right," the little one agreed, hoping thereby to avoid further questioning. "Can you tell us where we'll find 'em?"

"Last I saw of 'em they was squattin' way down Priddy Crick. Twenty-five mile from hyar. Seein' as how yo're greenhorns, yuh git lost shore as hell if I tried to direct yuh . . . See that saddle in the ridge east of hyar? Wal, yuh hit water, it'll be Priddy Crick. Go down it far enough and yuh'll find yore bunch."

Grumpy thanked him and waved him goodbye.

"He told us more'n he figgered," the little man remarked, as they headed for the ridge. "I reckon it's a party of engineers and surveyors the company's got in here. Been here some time, too."

Rainbow said it was no more than he expected.

Even before they found the creek, they heard blasting.

"That may come from some mine," said Rip, "but I don't

believe it; the explosions don't sound confined enough for that kind of work."

"You can say that again. Those shots didn't come from no mine; you don't fill a tunnel with fumes and dust at this time o'day." Grumpy touched his bronc with the spurs and proceeded up the slope directly ahead. Down below, he saw flowing water. "Here's yore crick!" he yelled back, turning in his saddle and gesturing to Rip and Bent.

They turned south, staying close to the stream but making no attempt at concealment.

"There's no reason why we should explain who we are and why we're here," said Rainbow.

It wasn't long before they saw the first stakes and little rock monuments of the preliminary survey that had been run well across Middle Park. After that, less than an hour's riding brought them up to a group of surveyors and their rodmen, who gave them a friendly greeting.

"If you boys are looking for work," one of them said, "see Sturdevant, back at camp; he's taking on all the men he can get and paying top wages."

"I don't believe we'd be interested," Rip told him. "But thanks just the same."

They reached the scene of the blasting and found that a deep cut was being blown through the solid rock shoulder of a mountain. Strung out toward Spanish Peak was a work force twice as large as the one toiling at Chipeta. No steel was being laid—that would come as soon as the tunnel through the Divide was completed and material could be brought in quickly and cheaply—but miles of roadbed were ready even now to receive it.

Rainbow had seen enough. According to his calculations—and they were based necessarily on newspaper reports of the progress being made in the tunnel—the Denver and Pacific would be at Mears Pass in another five to six weeks.

He discussed it freely with Grumpy and Bent, as they turned back. All they could do was to agree with him. What he had seen had a noticeably sobering effect on young Bent.

"I don't like to say it, Rip, but things look bad; they're going ahead just as though they had everything in the bag."

"They're certainly out to create that impression," said Rip. "We haven't seen anything over here that should discourage us. We know they're committed to going over Mears Pass. That's something we couldn't be sure of until now. I've always regarded the activity at Chipeta as a colossal bluff. I'm still of that opinion. With only five or six weeks to go, they don't want to do too much stalling about coming to us. If they do, they may find they're too late."

It was said so casually that it was a moment before its full import got through to Grumpy. When it did, he reared up and flicked a quick glance at Rainbow.

"What do you mean by that?" he demanded sharply.

"I'm not saying. But I've got something up my sleeve. I'll use it if I have to."

They spent the night east of the Pass. Early afternoon of the third day saw them moving down out of the hills above Dutch's ranch. They were still some distance from the house when they saw as many as ten horsemen pour into the road and set out for Lively at a swinging gallop. It pulled the partners and Bent to attention.

"What do you suppose is the meanin' of that?" the little one demanded anxiously. "That's more'n Dutch and his small crew."

"It is," Bent agreed. "Must be Lem Spade and some of his men in that bunch."

"Come on!" Rainbow exclaimed. "Let's get down to the house and find out what this is all about!"

CHAPTER 17

THE SOUND of their running ponies brought Dode Reedy, a banged-up old puncher who did the odd jobs on the ranch, to the door. Recognizing them, he shuffled out as they pounded into the yard.

"We saw Dutch and that bunch high-tailing it to town," Bent said. "What's wrong, Dode?"

"Plenty! Yuh didn't come down by way of Three Springs, did yuh?"

"No—"

"Wal, if yuh had, yuh'd have seen a certain party decoratin' the lower cottonwood."

"Who, Dode?"

"Why, the long-faced rat that Mark Curry turned out of jail. He wa'n't the only—"

"Wait a minute," Rainbow cut him off. "Suppose you begin at the beginning. You say Sawtelle's been strung up. I want to know why."

"Becuz we bin losin' beef, and so has Lem Spade—two and three head a night. Dutch and Lem got their facts straight before they did anythin'. There wa'n't no question but what the stuff was goin' into the pot, down there at Chipeta. I ain't namin' no names, but a bunch of men laid out around Three Springs last evenin', waitin' for them two-bit rustlers to show up.

"They didn't have to wait long. This fella Sawtelle and another one of them saloon gladiators moves down outa the hills and puts their ropes on a couple fat yearlin's. The boys shoulda busted 'em then and there, but they tried to close in. There was a runnin' fight. One of that pair got away. Sawtelle didn't. If they try their game ag'in, they'll git what he got."

Dode was properly indignant. The partners regarded each other solemnly.

"The two of us had the right hunch, Rip," Bent said.

"You did," Grumpy acknowledged. "I was wrong. But so were you, Rip; you figgered MacDonald would git Sawtelle outa the county in a hurry."

"This is a dirty business. Let's not waste breath on who was right and who was wrong." Rainbow's tone had a frosty edge. "Tell me, Dode—what are Dutch and Spade doing, racing to town in that fashion?"

"They aim to settle this thing with Curry. They're goin' to show him he can't turn any more of them wolves loose on the community. With all respect to you, Bent, yore old man's gone too far."

The tall man waited to hear no more. With a crisp command for Grumpy and Bent to get moving, he swung his bronc around and pulled it to a driving gallop. With Link incapacitated and themselves miles from town, he realized the desperateness of the situation. Coming on top of the past feeling against Curry, anything could happen. Grumpy and he needed Altmeyer and Spade. Crossing them would very likely cost their support.

Though there was no denying that the cowmen had a grievance against Curry, it did not call for the sort of violence that Dode had insinuated was to be meted out to him. Though the banker had put up Sawtelle's bail, it could have been arranged without his help, and undoubtedly would have been. Furthermore, Rip saw little reason to believe that the traffic in rustled beef would not have occurred if Sawtelle had remained in jail.

"This business was Shag's idea," he said to himself. "He didn't have to depend on Sawtelle; he had other men he could call on to do his raiding."

That the grim outcome of last night's adventure would deter Shag from further rustling was open to question. Rainbow gave little thought to that; his whole concern was for what the next hour or two might bring. He had no sympathy for Marcus Curry; but he had Bent and Jeannie to consider, and he knew he couldn't let them down, whatever the cost.

He turned in the saddle and beckoned for Grumpy to spur up beside him.

"This thing will go the way Lem Spade wants it to go! Don't pay too much attention to Dutch! Spade's the strong man! Understand?"

The little one nodded and drove on.

Their broncs were in a lather when they flashed into Lively. Down the street, they saw a crowd of at least a hundred people—men and women—gathered in front of the bank, which had already closed for the day. On the steps stood Link Easter, propped up on his crutches, a sawed-off shotgun in his hands. Curry was alone inside.

The partners and Bent swung down a few doors away and pushed through the rioting crowd. Many of the bank windows had been broken. As they reached Link's side, a rock crashed through still another, the glass showering them as it fell.

Link gave Rip and Grumpy a slitted glance. His leathery face was rocky.

"These dang fools have gone crazy, Rip! They can git away with stringin' up a rustler but they'll git Curry over my dead body!"

The tall man nodded. "We'll back you up on that. I don't

hold any brief for him but it won't help anybody to muss him up."

Lem Spade and Dutch shouldered their way up to the steps. Dutch started to spew out a torrent of wrath. Spade shut him up.

"Let me do the talkin'; we'll get somewheres, or I'll know it!" Lem glared at the partners. "I didn't expect to see you fellas linin' up against us! Where in hell do you stand, anyhow? Ain't that skunk in there done enough to you?"

"He's done plenty, Lem," Rainbow answered quietly. "But he's paying for it. If you want the truth, he's been mighty small potatoes for some time, as far as we're concerned . . . Dutch, you and Lem come up here; I've got something to say to you. The rest of you folks keep back; don't set foot on these steps."

Rainbow stepped close to the bank door with the two men. "If you got anythin' to say to us, you want to talk fast!" Dutch ripped out, his eyes wild and his face working nervously. "Come high, come low, we're goin' to git hold of that cuss inside and give him a dose of medicine he won't forgit!"

Rip ignored him and spoke to Spade.

"Lem, we're licked if we get martial law here, and that's exactly what we'll get if this mob has its way. If a company or two of Denver militia move in, you know whose side they'll be on. You'll lose more than a handful of cows, and so will we."

"Yo're wastin' yore time, Rip!" Spade declared adamantly. "Curry's goin' to pay for turnin' that rat loose on us!"

"Do you mean to tell me you figure Sawtelle would have stayed locked up if Curry hadn't gone to bat for him? You're wrong, if you do. The Denver and Pacific wouldn't have let that man come to trial; not with what we had on him. As for this rustling—how sure are you that they didn't run off some of his beef?"

"By God, I hope they did!" Dutch burst out again. "It would serve him right! He's done everybody dirt—started all this trouble! Gits me how you can say a word for him!"

"I'm not, Dutch; I'm just trying to tell you and Lem that Marcus Curry is a mighty small frog in this puddle. He bungled the sale of the Thunder River and Northern. That Denver crowd got through with him then and there. But they'll use him, if you'll give them the excuse. If that's what you want to do—go ahead. Pull down this bank; tear him limb from limb. But you'll have to climb over the four of us to get him."

The crowd had quieted for a minute or two, but it began to whoop it up again. Bent winced as another window was shattered. He had no enemies here, but had he stood there alone, he would most surely have been swept aside.

Rainbow caught his eye and beckoned him over.

"You better hear this, Bent. I still don't know what Lem and Dutch have in mind. If they whipped up this excitement in the hope that your father would be dragged out of the bank and beaten up or given a coat of tar, or worse, they know by now that they can't get away with it. But they want something. Do you mind saying what it is, Lem?"

Spade shifted his weight and exchanged an uneasy glance with Altmeyer. Now that it had been put up to them so bluntly, they didn't seem to know exactly what it was they wanted of Marcus Curry.

"Maybe you want him to shut up his bank and clear out of town," Rip suggested, taking advantage of their confusion.

"We need the bank," Lem muttered. "But he ain't goin' to pull no more of this stuff!" he added, with a sudden burst of hostility.

"Yo're dead right he ain't!" Dutch agreed. "If he wants to save his hide, let him agree to quit doin' the Denver and Pacific's dirty work! And we ain't takin' his word for it! We want some guarantee!"

"For instance?" Rainbow demanded.

"Let him put his ranch in Bent's name, with the understandin' that if we catch him dealin' from the bottom again that the property goes to the boy!"

"I don't know whether he'll agree to that or not. If he does, will that satisfy you, Lem?"

Spade signified that it would.

"All right," said Rip. "I'll put it up to him right now." It was only a step or two to the shattered front window. Reaching it, he called to Curry.

"I hear you!" came the flinty answer from inside. "I've heard every word that's been said out there!"

"I'm coming in," Rainbow told him. "You won't have to open the door; I'll knock out the rest of this glass and climb in through the window."

Curry had barricaded himself behind his desk, on which reposed a loaded shotgun and a brace of revolvers. He glared defiantly at Rip but there wasn't as much fight left in him as he pretended. His sagging jowls and wilted collar were proof enough that he had been badly shaken by the demonstration.

"Mr. Curry, this is the second time in a few days that you've had the wolves after you. Why don't you come to your senses and back out of this trouble as gracefully as you can?"

"Huh!" the other snorted contemptuously. "I didn't expect to hear anything as stupid as that from you, Ripley. How could I back out? I sold the railroad company an option on the Chipeta property for three times what it cost me. I put every dollar into Denver and Pacific stock. I've got everything else tied up in it. I couldn't let go if I wanted to—and I certainly don't want to. You and your partner will be at the end of your rope in a few weeks. The two of you have been investigated; the D. and P. knows what you're worth. You're operating on a shoestring."

"Certainly," Rainbow admitted. "No secret about that. But the Denver and Pacific is being a little premature if it thinks we're about ready to be swallowed at one gulp. I haven't heard it mentioned, Mr. Curry, but it's just possible that we have another customer for the Thunder River and Northern on the hook."

This was pure, unadulterated bluff on Rainbow's part.

When the blue chips were down, however, he could bluff with the best. His gray eyes were unreadable as he gazed across the desk at Curry, with a maddening smile of self-confidence playing over his wide mouth. Beset as the latter was with his own problems of the moment, he took the bait.

"What—the Midland?" He managed a jeering laugh. "I don't believe it! The Midland is broke! You'll have to tell that story to someone else; I don't believe it."

"That's your privilege," Rainbow conceded coolly. "I didn't say anything about the Midland. But just forget that I said anything at all." Feeling sure that the seed he had planted would bear fruit, he turned the conversation to the matter of the moment. "You know Bent is out there on the steps, ready to lay down his life to protect you. You must be a little proud of him."

"I am," Curry grunted. "I'll tell you, Ripley, the only regret I have is that I broke with the boy. You know I had nothing to do with running off those cows, or with anything else that's happened. You and your partner can take the responsibility for it; if you'd kept your fingers out of the pie, we'd all have been better off."

"I can't agree with you on that," Rip said flatly.

"I'm not asking you to agree with me!" was the violent retort. Curry pulled out a desk drawer and shoved a legal-looking document at the tall man. "I ain't backing down an inch for Lem Spade or Dutch Altmeyer—but there's a deed for the ranch. I want Bent to hold it. If anything happens to me, the property is his. I'll thank you now to get out of here. If Link Easter's got any authority left, he'll break up this mob and arrest some of these hoodlums."

Spade and Dutch chose to regard the outcome as a personal victory. The crowed listened to what the former had to say, but without being convinced that the show was over.

"We showed Mark Curry where he gits off!" Lem shouted. "I told you he'd put up the ranch as guarantee there'd be no more trouble from him! Now you folks break this up and go along home!"

A few left, but the crowd didn't really begin to disintegrate until after Spade and Dutch rode out of town, with their crews.

With a crutch stub, Link cleared a space on the steps of broken glass and rubbish and sat down wearily. He had been standing there for an hour.

"You all right?" Grumpy asked. "You look a little white around the gills."

"This dang leg's stiff as a board, but I'm okay. You fellas was shore a fine sight for sore eyes. I wouldn't have dared to use my gun. I knew if blood was spilled that those fools would go wild and pull me down before I could say Jack Robinson."

"Where was Charlie Hughes? Why wasn't he here with you, Link?"

"I gave him the day off; he's down at the Junction with his missus." The old man pulled out a package of Mail Pouch and popped a generous wad of tobacco into his mouth. "I got business at Three Springs. Charlie'll have to drive me out tonight."

Save for the very old and the very young, the crowd had left. Rainbow surveyed the damage done to the building.

"Your father will have to get Bud Wilkenson or someone to board up the windows till new glass can be put in," he told Bent. "It might be a good idea for you to wait here and walk him home. I don't think it's necessary, but he'll appreciate it."

Bent nodded soberly. "I'll be glad to. I want to thank you for everything, Rip. The jig would have been up but for you. What did he say when he handed you the deed to the ranch?"

"That he wanted you to have the spread if anything happened to him. It was all signed. He just reached into his desk for it and handed it to me."

Bent pondered over it for a moment or two, his young face furrowed with his thinking. Hopefully, he said, "He must be weakening, Rip."

"He knows he's made some mistakes. But don't get the idea that he's coming over on our side. I'm counting on the fact that he won't. I want him to stand pat. He'll do us more good than harm."

It was a baffling remark. Bent didn't understand, and he said so.

"Don't worry about it," Rainbow said lightly. "I gave your father some information that I want the Denver and Pacific to get. I'm sure he'll send it along to them."

CHAPTER 18

THE FOLLOWING day was Sunday. It was quiet in Lively. Though the news that the partners brought back from Middle Park, as well as the trouble at the bank and what had led to it, gave Jeannie little to celebrate, it was her birthday, and she invited Rip, Grumpy and Bent to the house for dinner.

It was a comfortable old place, with an enormous back yard. The apple trees were in blossom. The blue sky was cloudless, with only the faintest breath of wind stirring. On such a day, it was pleasant to sit there and drink in the fragrance of blossoms and listen to the music of the bees.

A number of Jeannie's friends dropped in during the afternoon and stayed a few minutes. Amid the coming and going, Con Hanrahan, tall and straight in his Sunday-best, came up the front walk and followed a worn and familiar path around the house to the back yard, his step light and springy. As always on such occasions, he had a gift for Jeannie.

"It ain't much," he told her. "Just a little something I got for you the other day when I was down to the Junction."

"What a beautiful comb, Con!" she exclaimed, on opening

the package. "You never forget me!" Her eyes were suddenly misty. "You sit down here with Grumpy; I want you to have a piece of my cake and some coffee."

She hurried into the house.

"You look like yoreself again, with that bandage off your head," Grumpy observed, as Con settled himself on the rustic bench. "Reckon you won't shed no tears over Ike Sawtelle."

"Not a wan! Me only regret is that the county will be put to the expense of burying him."

After exchanging a word or two with Rainbow and Bent, he said to the latter, "Why don't you step into the kitchen and give Jeannie a hand with the coffee? Tell her no fussing on my account."

He was so casual about it that Bent obliged without suspecting that Con was getting rid of him.

"I didn't want to mention this in front of Bent," Con explained, as soon as he was alone with the partners. "On the way over, I saw Marcus Curry driving out of town, headed for Chipeta. I wasn't the only man who saw him. After what happened yesterday you'd think the man would go a little slow in his hobnobbing with Ambrose MacDonald."

"He has an important message to deliver, Con," Rainbow observed with obvious satisfaction.

"Shure and you sound as though you knew what it was."

"I should know," Rip declared, with a smile. "I put a bug in his ear yesterday. I'm not surprised that he's losing no time about passing it on to MacDonald."

This was news to Grumpy. He straightened up, a question on his lips. Jeannie and Bent came out at the moment, however, and it was not until he was alone with Rip that evening that he got around to demanding an explanation.

"Don't be so testy about it," Rainbow told him. "Your curiosity has been tormenting you something terrible ever since I made that remark this afternoon."

"And why not? You've been makin' a lot of mysterious cracks of late, like tellin' Bent the other day that if the Denver and Pacific stalled too long they might find themselves too late. You've been up to somethin'."

"I certainly have, Grump. It's been all I could do to keep you from knowing that the Judge and I have been corresponding almost daily for the past two weeks."

"Hell's fire!" the little one exploded cantankerously. "Do you mean to tell me you been goin' behind my back and puttin' somethin' over with Judge Carver without lettin' me in on it?"

"I have. I didn't intend to say anything to you until it was all set. Now that you've brought it up, I'll have to tell you. Close the window; this thing isn't worth a plugged nickel unless there's absolute secrecy. I'm warning you, Grumpy, not even Jeannie can be let in on it. You may not like the deception we'll have to practice on her and Bent and Con and all the rest of them. I don't like it myself, but that's the only way it will pay off."

"For Pete's sake, will you stop that line of talk and git down to cases?" the little one snapped.

"Very well. Let's go 'way back. You know the Union Pacific is poison to the D. and P., and that's been so for years. If you want to throw a scare into that Denver crowd, just say Union Pacific. Can you imagine the scurrying around little Ambrose MacDonald would be doing if he got the idea that the U.P. was interested in taking over the Thunder River and Northern, or in putting up the money so we could build up through Painted Meadows and meet them coming down from Rawlins?"

"Yeh, I can imagine it—and that's all I can do," said the little man. "It don't make sense. You heard what Con had to say about buildin' up that way to support a railroad."

"He was talking about one thing and I'm talking about another. For us to extend a narrow gauge road up through the Meadows wouldn't fool anyone. It would be something else for the U.P. to come down on a standard gauge road and drive right into the heart of Denver and Pacific territory."

Grumpy shook his head incredulously. "Rip, you know they're not going to do it."

"Of course they're not, but we're going to make them believe that's the program. Judge Carver has done some tremendous favors for the Union Pacific. I told him what I had in mind and asked him if he could get some U.P. bigwig to come down and pretend to look things over—somebody so big that Ambrose MacDonald would take notice. To make it even better, I suggested that whoever came down would slip into Lively quietly, register under an assumed name and give MacDonald the idea that he was trying to cover up his business here . . . Well, the Judge has arranged it; Henry Moulton has agreed to needle the Denver and Pacific for us. All that remains to be settled is when he can get here."

"Moulton," the little one gasped. "They don't come any bigger; I can't believe it, Rip!"

"There's a reason, of course. Moulton and the Denver and Pacific had some trouble about terminal facilities in Denver last summer. MacDonald was in on that, the Judge says. This will give Moulton a chance to pay off an old score. If you need a bigger reason, the U.P. wants to keep its Salt Lake business. This cut-off will drain away some of it."

Rainbow sat back, enjoying Grumpy's amazement.

"Well, what have you got to say, Grump? You know we'll have to play it to the hilt and make Jeannie and the others believe it's on the level."

Grumpy weighed it soberly.

"Can we git away with it, Rip?"

"We'll have to. There's a fight coming in Ute Canyon that'll make hash of our legal rights. We'll have to throw every man we can muster into it. MacDonald will go all out. Maybe we can stand him off. But that won't be enough. They'll wear us down in time. Curry admitted to me yesterday that we'd be investigated. They know to the dollar how much money we've got. It'll change the whole picture if we can make them think the U.P. is interested."

"Is that what you hinted to Curry?"

"I suggested that we might have someone else on the hook. He thought I meant the Midland. MacDonald will know better. I predict that he'll go down to White River Junction in the morning and get some wires off to Denver."

"I'll make it my business to find out if he does," the little one declared. "Con's got a carload of ties to bring down tomorrow. I'll go down with him on Number 3 and lay over on the Y till the mornin' train passes."

His resentment at having been left out of Rainbow's scheming rapidly disappeared. He admitted that he would have opposed the idea had it been put up to him.

"I'd say you were crazy, Rip. Now that you've put it over, I know it's the smartest thing we could have done. How you goin' to break this to Jeannie?"

"I'm not going to say a word till Moulton gets here. It may be a week or ten days."

The bank opened on time on Monday morning. Curry had had the debris cleared away. Two men were at work installing new glass.

During the course of the morning Ike Sawtelle was interred in an unmarked grave in the Lively cemetery. There were no mourners. Link came down to the depot afterwards. He had dispensed with one crutch.

"I'll throw the other one away tomorrow," he told Jeannie and Rip. "The leg don't pain any. Jest a mite stiff. See a couple wagons in town for supplies as usual. Reckon the camp will be buyin' more meat in Lively than it has been. Where's Bent?"

"He's down below, keeping an eye on the canyon," Rip told him.

"Mark stopped me as I was passin' the bank. Wanted to know if I'd ever heard you say anythin' about the Midland wantin' the narrow gauge. Said you'd told him they did."

"I told him nothing of the sort," Rainbow protested. "If he wants to put that interpretation on it, let him. He's had the idea right along that no one but the Denver and Pacific had any interest in the road. He may be mistaken."

"You mean that, Rainbow?" Jeannie was quick to ask.

"Certainly I mean it."

"You've been dickering with someone?"

"Jeannie, I'm not going to say yes or no to that. But I'll

tell you this much: Curry and the rest of that crowd are going to find that we haven't put all our eggs in one basket."

Grumpy and Con were back in town before noon. The little one got Rip's ear.

"You were right, Rip; MacDonald flagged the down train. He was out early, so he'd be shore not to miss it."

"Good," said Rainbow. "Maybe we'll be hearing from him in a day or two."

With the arrival of the evening train, they learned from Pop Burke, the conductor, that Ambrose MacDonald had returned to Chipeta.

"He wasn't gone long," Rip commented. "I didn't think he would be."

There was a letter for him, but it was from Ferris Greenwood, not from Moulton, as he expected. He read the letter and passed it over to Grumpy. It concerned another bank robbery.

"No chance of our rushing out to Idaho on a case right now," said Grumpy. "You better wire him before Jeannie leaves for the night."

Rip rather expected that MacDonald would look him up the following day and make him an offer, however unacceptable. That didn't prove to be the case. But late in the afternoon, Bent arrived with news that MacDonald's surveyors had staked out a crossing of the T. R. and N. tracks and after proceeding up the slope on which the tie-spur was located had turned up the west wall of the canyon.

"You know there's places where there seems to be a sort of ledge along the west wall, a couple hundred feet below the rim," Bent explained. "They lowered men on ropes and got a transit down there. There's places where a man can't find any footing at all. They skipped those spots and worked all afternoon. You'll see the marks they left—daubs of white paint."

"So you figure they're going to blast out a roadbed high above the river, eh?" Rip asked. He took it so calmly that Grumpy was instantly annoyed.

"What would you figger?" he demanded hotly. "They ain't up there to do a circus act!"

"I don't suppose they are." Rainbow refused to get excited. "I know the ledge Bent speaks of. A goat couldn't negotiate it, let alone a railroad. This is just another trick to bring us to terms."

Con Hanrahan came in. Rainbow put the matter up to him. "Can they do it, Con?"

"Shure they can, if they don't care how much it costs or how long it takes. They'd have to blast out a shelf ten feet wide. If they worked from both ends, the job would take thim a year. The cost would run into millions. But, if you ask me, that ain't their game, Rip; pretending to build a roadbed up there will give thim an excuse for their blasting. The first shot may put us out of business."

"How do you figger that?" Grumpy demanded.

"Huh! Shure and what do you think is going to happen to the rock they rip out? It'll plunge into the river and over our tracks. If a train is caught in the canyon, it'll be curtains for it. And how long do you think it would be before all that rock raises the river level and drowns us out?"

"You're right," Rainbow agreed soberly. "I called it a trick. I was wrong; this is their big move. We'll have to stop them, or we're through!"

"How do you propose to go about it?" queried Bent. "The law won't help us. They'll buy all the law they need to put them in the clear."

"We'll have to wolf our way through this," Rip said tightly. "If MacDonald doesn't come to see me in the morning, I'll go down to Chipeta to see him."

Ambrose MacDonald drove into Lively shortly after nine, the next day. He was there expressly to see the partners, but he pretended to have other business, in the course of which he spent some time with Marcus Curry. As a consequence, it was nearing noon when he walked into the depot. Rainbow was alone in the office, Jeannie having just left for lunch. Grumpy had gone down to the canyon with Bent to observe what was being done there. The day was so warm that Rip

had propped the office door open. Through it, he saw
MacDonald the moment he stepped into the waiting room. It
gave him a second or two to gird his loins.

"Mr. Ripley, I'm Ambrose MacDonald," his visitor announced, his tone suggesting that this was just another routine
business call and completely ignoring the past and prospective
strife in which they were engaged.

"I had a faint suspicion that you were," Rip returned, with
a straight face. With elaborate courtesy, he indicated a chair
and invited MacDonald to sit down. "Now that we know each
other," he continued, "may I inquire what I can do for you?"

The latter sized him up carefully and decided that the kid
glove approach he had been using might better be forgotten.

"Ripley, I'm here to talk business." Little Ambrose
MacDonald was his hard-hitting self now. "You're aware that
we are exploiting the possibilities of going down the west
wall of Ute Canyon, high above the river. We think it's fea-
sible. I don't have to tell you it will be expensive."

He got no help from Rainbow, who listened and had no
comment to offer. It was a familiar bit of strategy that
MacDonald had often used himself.

"I know Ketchel made you several offers for T. R. and
N.," he went on after a moment's hesitation. "I understand
his best offer was fifty thousand. Am I right about that?"

Rip nodded. "I believe that was the figure."

MacDonald clipped the end off an expensive cigar with a
gold clipper that he wore attached to his watch chain. He put
the cigar into his mouth but did not light it, something he
never did. He did not smoke; a cigar with him was a sort of
licorice stick on which he sucked until it was shredded, when
a fresh one took its place.

"Ripley"—his eyes were as vacant as an Indian's as he
spoke—"I wonder if you'd change your mind if I doubled
that offer."

The tall man smiled with an obscure amusement.

"Mr. MacDonald, you've got a low opinion of my mind
if you think that would change it."

"My God, Ripley, how much do you expect to squeeze

out of this junk heap?" the other exclaimed, his patience at an end. "Your partner bought it for next to nothing."

"I'll answer that by asking you a question," Rainbow returned. "How much would you say the Denver and Pacific would attempt to squeeze out of it if our positions were reversed?"

"That's a very humorous observation," MacDonald declared, with a sarcastic chuckle. "I must remember to try that on Alvin Ketchel. But that's beside the point, Ripley. You've got your price. What is it?"

"Any price we'd accept would have a string on it. You know what it is. We feel we owe something to these people. We're not going to see Lively turned into a ghost town just to further enrich the Denver and Pacific. Your engineers have found the old Ute trail that runs over Mears Pass. It would be a simple matter for you to follow it into Lively. It would add very little to your total mileage. Whenever you're ready to make that a condition of your bid, we'll be happy to listen to you, and not before."

MacDonald tossed his frayed cigar into a wastebasket. In his most precise manner, he said, "I'm afraid you'll wait a long while."

"Not too long," was Rainbow's confident answer. "Lively will have a standard gauge railroad that will put it in touch with the rest of the world. If the D. and P. doesn't build it, someone else will. And I'm not alluding to the Colorado Midland, as Curry may have suggested to you."

Seasoned warrior that he was, Ambrose MacDonald had to admire the tall man's poise and shrewdness. Snapping to his feet, he said, "That leaves only the Union Pacific. You wouldn't go so far as to tell me the U.P. is considering building down here from Wyoming, would you?"

Rip met it with a bland, inscrutable smile.

"I prefer to let events speak for themselves. Suppose we leave it at that."

MacDonald started out, only to turn at the door.

"You don't know what you're letting yourself in for, Ripley. I've been through these things before, and I haven't got the reputation of coming off second best. We'll be over Mears Pass in a month. I can't hold off any longer; I've got to go after you."

"By blowing rock off that west wall and blocking our roadbed and endangering the lives of our crew and passengers? When that happens, you won't see us turning to the courts to get mired in one of your legal swamps; you'll get our answer in a hurry, and you'll get it direct."

CHAPTER 19

RAINBOW WAS careful to tell Jeannie only as much as he wanted her to know of what had passed between MacDonald and himself. She realized that the showdown was at hand.

"Haven't you closed the door on further negotiations?" she asked, after thinking over what he had said.

"If we show him that we can stand him off, he'll be back. He's ready to lead his high card, and we'll have to top it. I'm going to spend the afternoon out in the Meadows. A few weeks ago, Spade and Corbett and the rest of them were ready to go all out to help us. The rustling has been put down, but that trouble at the bank may have taken the edge off their enthusiasm. I've got to find out. You can tell Grump and Bent that I had a talk with MacDonald. I expect they'll be here before I get back. If so, I'll see them at the hotel."

Aside from Dutch Altmeyer, he found the Painted Meadows cowmen no less ready to throw themselves and their crews into the fight than they had been.

"You leave Dutch to me," Spade told him. "He's a stubborn

Dutchman, but I can handle him. He knows yore slant on that trouble with Curry was the right one. I'll talk to him."

He had supper with Lem and his wife. When he got back to town, it was after nine. Grumpy and Bent were upstairs, waiting for him.

"Before you start firing questions at me," he advised, "tell me what happened down in the canyon today."

"The surveyors was crawling all over that west wall," said Grumpy. "One of the foremen had a gang workin' on the slope, close to the tie spur, hackin' out a road. Reckon they're gittin' ready to drag a gas engine and a compressor up there. Shag and his gang was hangin' around, lookin' for trouble. I'm tellin' you, we ain't helpin' ourselves none by waitin'. The sooner we git up there on the rim, with a bunch of men we can depend on, the better off we'll be . . . How did you find things out in the Meadows?"

"All right. All we've got to do is pass the word and we'll have all the men we need. But I'm not going to send them into this fight and run the risk of stopping a slug until MacDonald actually starts blasting rock down on us."

"By grab, you won't have to wait long!" the little one growled. "Don't you be surprised if Number 2 ain't able to git up the canyon tomorrow evenin'!"

"Possibly not," Rainbow agreed soberly. "The three of us will go down with Con after the morning train pulls out. We'll stand on the Y all day and see how things go."

After Bent left, Grumpy demanded a fuller account of what MacDonald's visit had developed than Jeannie had been able to give him. Rip told him in detail.

"Did that Union Pacific angle jar him any?"

Rainbow smiled thinly. "He's a good poker player, Grump. I didn't expect him to fall apart. But what do you think brought him in to see me if it wasn't that? If Moulton showed up tomorrow, I believe Ambrose MacDonald would throw in the towel. It's too early to be looking for Moulton. But a couple days, one way or the other, may make a whale of a difference to us."

When Con ran Number 3 into the Chipeta Y, next morning,

upwards of a hundred laborers were already at work on the road over which MacDonald obviously intended to haul heavy equipment up to the west wall. The course it was to take was clearly indicated. After heading away from the tie spur for three hundred yards, to gain elevation, it described a sharp curve and swung back to the river.

"They'll never haul a train up that grade," Con declared emphatically. "It's too steep for even wan of thim big Diesel jobs."

Shag and his gunmen were in evidence, but they did no work, other than moving around with the sun so as to keep in the shade. So far as the partners could see, Ambrose MacDonald remained in the headquarters tent.

"Reckon he figgers his construction boss can handle this job," Grumpy observed. "It'll take 'em a couple days, Rip."

"It should," the tall man agreed. "We'll stick it out, no matter how long it takes."

Some blasting was done during the afternoon, the rock being used for fill. Toward evening, Number 2 came chuffing up the canyon and ran by Chipeta without stopping. Half an hour later, work on the slope stopped for the day. The men trooped back to camp, with the teamsters and the mules bringing up the rear.

The following day was a repetition of the first.

"They'll hit the wall in the mornin'," Grumpy remarked that night, as he pulled off his boots and prepared for bed. "A couple days gone, and still no sign of Moulton. It's beginnin' to look to me as though he might show up too late to do us any good."

"Stop your croaking," said Rainbow. "I'm going to sit up and read the papers."

He found some news of more than passing interest. The Spanish Peak tunnel was so near to completion that the Denver and Pacific was arranging a celebration to signalize the piercing of the Divide. Railroad and political dignitaries had been invited. A short stretch of track on the western slope was already completed, and the Governor, it said, would be at the throttle of the first train through.

It brought home to Rip how great were the odds against which Grumpy and he were fighting. But a thought occurred to him that made him smile.

"That's right," he mused; "Moulton is sure to see this. Better than anything else it will tell him how urgently we need him."

Ambrose MacDonald's drillers attacked the west wall shortly after noon, next day. The power-driven diamond bits sank into the red granite at the rate of two to three inches a minute. As soon as the first series of borings was completed, charges were placed in them and exploded immediately. The earth trembled and tons of rock, sheared off the wall, rose lazily into the air and then hurtled downward into the river, geysers of water shooting into the air where the pieces struck. Jagged fragments dug into the roadbed and bounced off the ties and rails.

"Is that enough for you?" Grumpy jerked out fiercely.

"More than enough," was Rip's toneless answer. His face had whipped hard and flat in its peculiar way. "They'll send down a lot more rock before they knock off for the day. We'll have to clear the stuff away. We can roll most of it into the river. I see one chunk that we'll have to put a chain on and use the engine to move it."

Grumpy stared at him aghast.

"You wanta git killed? That's what you'll be askin' for if you git caught down there when a blast goes off!"

"Number 2 will be along in a few hours. I'm not going to see her bottled up in Ute Canyon. We'll get her through and cancel all trains till this thing's decided one way or the other."

The little man offered no further argument.

"I forgot about Number 2," he growled. "I'd like to be up there on the rim with a rifle. I'd stop that bunch single-handed!"

Con walked out on the running board of the engine and took a long look down the canyon. His rawboned face was grim when he returned to the cab.

"It'll be a miracle if that big niggerhead didn't flatten a rail. Like I said, the river's boiling up behind all that rock. If they keep dumping it in, it won't be long before we'll be under water all the way down the canyon."

The drills were soon biting into the wall again. An hour later, another half-dozen shots were detonated. Again rock rained down into the river and over the T. R. and N. tracks. Up on the ledge, men swarmed back to work as soon as the wind carried the dust away. With crowbars, they loosened great pieces of the fractured granite and sent them crashing into the canyon. Soon the drills were clattering once more.

Rainbow winced. To stand idly by, without lifting even a protesting finger, was a punishing experience. But he did not waver in his resolve to get Number 2 through. That was the first thing to do.

"They're having it all their way today," he said to himself. "We'll have something to say about how things go tomorrow."

Grumpy studied his watch soberly.

"They'll touch off another round up there before they quit for the day. If it takes 'em as long to git ready this time as last, Number 2 will jest about run into it."

"We'll see that she doesn't," Rip replied. "You and Bent come with me. We'll go down the canyon now and flag her."

"Barney and me can run you down," Con offered.

"No, you set right here with Number 3. I'll take no chance on having everything we've got tied up. When we start clearing that stuff out of the way, I'll have Junie give you three toots of the whistle. Don't come down till you hear him calling you."

They were seen from above as they moved down the tracks. Someone up above hurled a rock at them. It struck the east wall several feet above their heads and ricocheted into the river. Grumpy's hand flashed to his gun.

"Don't try it!" Rip warned. "Start anything like that and we'll be dead bait in a hurry!"

They reached the big slab of granite that had splintered several ties and come to rest squarely between the tracks. Bent examined the outside rail.

"It's split a bit," he announced. "Do you think Number 2 can crawl over it?"

"If Dennis takes it easy," Rip said, after taking a look at the damaged rail. Grimly, he added, "No telling what the next blast will do to us."

They proceeded down the canyon for half a mile and waited there for the up train. Dennis Rafferty, the engineer, recognized them and slapped on the air at once. Pop Burke, the conductor, came running up to get an explanation for this unexpected stop.

Rainbow told the train crew what the situation was.

"How many passengers are you carrying, Pop?"

"Three or four women and youngsters and about the same number of men."

"We'll have to ask the men to give us a hand when we start clearing away."

T. R. and N. passengers were used to pitching in and helping to get a train through. On one occasion they had toiled for two days, and in bitter weather, digging out of a snowslide.

The minutes ticked away as the train stood there. Grumpy consulted his watch again.

"Gittin' late," he said. "They've had time enough to set off another round. Do you suppose the skunks are waitin' for us to show up, so they can give it to us right in the face?"

Rainbow did not attempt an answer. Five minutes later the rolling thunder of an explosion reached them, echoing and reechoing as it moved down the canyon.

"There it is!" Grumpy growled. "Reckon we can be movin'."

"It didn't sound as heavy to me as the first two," said Rip. "Maybe it wouldn't, this far away. You get in the cab, Bent. Grump and I will ride the pilot. You'll see the rock that's fallen on the track, Dennis. Run up as close as you think safe. We'll go to work, then. If it looks as though they'd knocked off for the day, up there, I'll have you signal Con to run down Junie, and put a chain on the heaviest stuff."

They reached the scene of the blasting. Work on the wall

seemed to be over for the day; men and mules were moving back to camp. Con was called down with Number 3, and all hands began clearing away the debris that littered the tracks.

The big niggerhead was rolled into the river without too much difficulty. The smaller stuff was no problem. Then with the job almost finished, another blast tore jagged pieces of rock out of the wall. No order was necessary to send passengers and train crew scurrying to cover behind the engines. A boulder as large as a man's head crashed through the roof of the combination day coach. Smaller fragments shattered most of its windows on the river side.

"The murthering scuts!" Con raged. "That was deliberate! No accidental delayed shots about it! I told Barney that last round sounded light!"

"I thought so, too!" Rip agreed. "It'll be a miracle if someone in the coach wasn't killed!"

They ran up the steps to investigate. A woman and a child of twelve had been injured, the woman seriously. The injured were unknown to the partners.

"George Warren's wife and little girl," Bent told them. "Mrs. Warren's Lem Spade's sister."

The other women, panic-stricken for a minute, came to the aid of Mrs. Warren and her daughter. The important thing to do now was to clear the tracks again and get the injured to town.

The job was done in less than half an hour. Number 3 ran back to the Y. With the road open, the train felt its way over the damaged rail. Rafferty opened the throttle then. Twelve minutes later, Number 2 rolled into Lively, her whistle screaming a frantic summons that brought half the town to the depot to meet her.

Eliza Warren died that evening. The wantonness with which she and her daughter had been struck down, to say nothing of the equal danger to which the others on the train had been subjected, sent a tidal wave of wrath and indignation rolling over Lively. Even Marcus Curry raised his voice against the Denver and Pacific.

Rainbow and Grumpy had just finished a quick supper and

were going up to their rooms when Curry burst into the hotel and overtook them on the stairs. His usually stony face was flushed with excitement.

"I've got no apologies to offer for anything I've done. I figure a man's got a right to make money if he can. But the D. and P.'s gone too far. When they begin making war on women and children, I quit. I'm ready to go down to Chipeta with you right now and demand at gunpoint that Ambrose MacDonald turn over to us the man or men responsible for this outrage."

"I'm glad you've seen the light," said Rip, as he mastered his surprise. "The best thing you can do, Mr. Curry, is to come up to our rooms and stay there. This town's a powder keg with a lighted fuse this evening. I wouldn't guarantee your safety if you're caught on the street. Bent's out in the valley right now, rounding up the men we want. We'll be ready to ride before midnight. And I don't mind telling you it's not our intention to waste any time talking to Ambrose MacDonald."

Over his protests, they got him upstairs.

"Is Bent going to the Curry ranch—to C Bar—for men?" he demanded.

"I don't believe he is," said Rainbow. "We can get along without your men."

"They're experienced men!" Curry insisted. "They won't wilt under gunsmoke. You get word to them! Tell them I said they're to go with Bent."

"We'll try," Rainbow promised. "You keep the door locked now."

"Be shore you do." Grumpy seconded. "There ain't no one in Lively who'll listen to an explanation from you to-night!"

After dispatching a messenger to C Bar, with Curry's instructions, the partners started for Link Easter's barn to get their horses. They slipped past the sheriff's office, saddled up and were beginning to think they might be able to get out of town without encountering the old man, thereby avoiding any discussion of their plans, to which he well might make violent objection. On reaching the street, however, they found Link blocking the alley entrance.

"Jest a minit!" he barked. "I wanta talk to you boys!"

The partners pulled up at once.

"Hear yo're organizin' to go after that gang of wolves at Chipeta," Link began again.

"We're organizing to protect our property," Rip returned.

"Huh!" old Link snorted. "That's the same thing—or it'll soon git to be the same thing! If you ain't aimin' to take the law into yore own hands, why you been steerin' clear of me this evenin'?"

"Link, the only charge you can bring against MacDonald is criminal negligence. And you'll have to prove that." Rip had never advanced an argument with greater earnestness. "You'll do yourself and everybody else a favor if you'll just look the other way for a few hours."

"I'll do nothin' of the sort!" was the flinty answer. "You can call killin' an innocent woman and cripplin' a child criminal negligence if you want. That gang saw the train standin' down there. They knew what they was doin'. I call it premeditated murder. I've got the authority to deputize as many men as I see fit in an emergency. That's what I'm goin' to do. I'm orderin' you right now to have a train standin' by with steam up to get us down to Chipeta in the next hour."

"Let me ask him a question," Grumpy interjected as Rainbow would have replied. "Link—you know MacDonald's got spies here in Lively. He knows what's goin' on here tonight; nobody's goin' to take that outfit by surprise . . . Are you jest goin' to bust in down there, or have you got somethin' worked out?"

"I'm takin' possession of that west wall. If I find 'em up there tonight, I'll order 'em off. I won't argue the matter; they'll go or stop lead. There'll be no more blastin' in Ute Canyon as long as I represent the law around here!"

It was the very action the partners proposed to take.

Rip said, "I don't know how long you can make it stick, Link; but it's good enough for us."

He was quick to realize the advantage of casting the mantle of the law over his followers.

"We'll have between forty and fifty men on the flats east of town between now and midnight," he continued. "Why not deputize them and ride with us, Link?"

"I will on one condition."

"Name it."

"You boys and Spade and the rest are to take orders from me."

Grumpy nodded and Rainbow said, "That will be all right with us, Link."

CHAPTER 20

IT WAS AFTER midnight when Link led his little army of deputies across the Meadows into the San Cristobal foothills. It was his intention to cut through the hills above the tie camp and reach the rim of Ute Canyon some distance below the scene of the blasting operations.

"We couldn't have suggested anything better," Rainbow told Bent. "I've never been along that rim, but if it's anything like a hundred others I've seen, there must be some cover up there."

"The rock cap is weathered and crisscrossed with deep cracks. A man on foot can crawl along most anywhere. It's no place for horses, Rip. We'll have to leave our broncs in the timber."

Bent had four of his old C Bar riders with him. They were seasoned men. Two of them, Chick Bannon and Bib Failes, had taught him most of what he knew about the cattle business.

Cowboys and owners, Dutch Altmeyer among them, representing more than a dozen brands, rode with the partners tonight. Lem Spade had sent his entire crew. He'd have been there himself but for his wife's violent insistence that if he had any respect for his dead sister he would see her laid in her grave before he went busting off with a gun in his fist.

"He's been carryin' on like a wild man, I hear," Grumpy commented. "Mebbe it's jest as well he ain't with us. We ain't off on no picnic, I'm tellin' you!"

The night was still and bright. The moon had risen so late that men and horses cast their shadows ahead and could not overtake them. The drone of voices mingled with the champing of the horses and the creaking of riding gear.

There was talk about Marcus Curry. Dutch insisted that it was a hoax; that Curry would never split with the Denver and Pacific. Uncle Joe Corbett and many others thought differently.

"You could hear Dutch a mile off," Grumpy protested.

"Don't let it bother you," said Rip. "There's no chance of taking that crowd by surprise. MacDonald knows what the score is. That blast wouldn't have been set off this evening if he hadn't calculated the odds and convinced himself that he could get away with it. I'll be surprised if he hasn't armed every man in camp."

They left the valley floor presently and began climbing. These foothills had been timbered off in the long ago. Left to themselves, they had gone back to tangled scrub and impenetrable patches of buckbrush. Link didn't bother to give it a thought. He found the trail he wanted. It didn't promise much, but he turned into it and bade the others to follow. Stretched out in single file, they toiled along after him and in less than an hour reached big timber and comparatively easy going.

Rip judged that they were now in back of the tie camp and well above it. Word had been sent to Jim Flynn, instructing him to be on the alert.

"Still down there," Grumpy observed. "Not a light showin'. Jim's usin' his head. Reckon he's got a job on his hands, explainin' to his gang why they ain't in this fight."

"It's not over yet," said Rip. "They may be in it plenty."

The course Link was setting began to take them off to the east. Presently, the timber began to thin, hinting that they were coming out on the Ute Canyon rim. Another thirty minutes passed, however, before the sheriff called a halt. As Bent had predicted, Link ordered the horses left in the timber, with two men detailed to stand guard over them.

He called the members of the posse around him.

"Before we start workin' up the rim, there's a thing or two I wanta say to you. The sun gits up early these June mornin's. In another forty-five minutes, we'll be able to see what we're up against. I warned you before we set out, and I'm tellin' you ag'in, and for the last time: there ain't to be no shootin' unless I tell you to shoot. If someone or t'other of you figgers he can't git out there without blastin' away at the first thing that moves, he better sit it out right here."

"He's talkin' to you, Dutch!" one of Spade's punchers taunted, knowing how easy it was to needle Altmeyer.

"I'm talkin' to every last one of you!" Link retorted, his voice as rasping as a rusty saw. "If a bunch of them railroad fellas has forted up along the west wall, I'll give 'em a chance to clear out; and that's all I will give 'em. If they won't go peaceably, then it'll be time enough to get tough with 'em."

"Reckon they'll be pumpin' lead at us before yo're finally convinced that they mean business!" Grumpy objected strenuously. "If they're up here, they've dug in, and they ain't goin' to be talked into pullin' out."

It won the muttered approval of the valley men. The sheriff bristled resentfully.

"I'm givin' orders here," he growled. "We'll play it my way."

"That's all right," Uncle Joe Corbett declared, "but there ain't no reason why we should sit here till dawn to find out what we're up against. I'm ready to make a little scout along this rim."

"I'll go with you," Rip volunteered at once, adding "that's if Link has no objection."

Thus did he hope to smooth the old man's ruffled feelings. He was convinced a brief reconnaissance would reveal that

MacDonald's men were on the rim, with his main force established on the improvised road leading up to the ledge where the blasting was being done. He was just as sure that any attempt to parley with them would come to nothing. But if the sheriff wanted to try, Rip saw no reason to object.

Link surprised him, and Grumpy even more, by saying, "Rip, I'll tag along with you and Uncle Joe. I'm still draggin' my leg a bit, but I can make it. Grumpy, you stick here and take charge. If you hear any shootin', it'll mean we've run into trouble. You come quick."

The little man didn't relish the idea of being left behind; but he had turned the tables on himself and couldn't do anything about it.

Rainbow crossed to the lip of the rim. Deep in its gorge, he could see Thunder River running white. He waited there until Uncle Joe was in position, to his left, and Link began to work up between them.

By taking advantage of every crevasse and pile of scattered malpais, and advancing on hands and knees when no protection at all offered, they moved along the rim for a thousand yards without encountering the faintest sign of anyone. Then, without warning, a rifle cracked on the lip of the rim, far ahead of Rainbow. With a wicked spang-g-g the slug whined over his head. A shallow crevice opened before him. He leaped into it and flattened out as a second shot pinged off the rock where he had stood but a moment before.

Uncle Joe Corbett had caught the second muzzle flash as he crawled around a reef of decaying quartz. Without waiting for anyone's permission, he flung his rifle to his shoulder and emptied a clip of cartridges at the spot where the night had blossomed red for a split second. Slugs began to sting the rocks around about him as viciously as though he had upset a hornet's nest.

Rip and Link made their way over to Uncle Joe and found he hadn't received a scratch. But he was annoyed.

"Reckon that settles a couple things for you, Link!" he ripped out hotly. "They're up here, spoilin' for a fight. They ain't goin' to listen to any of yore jawbone, and you know it!"

"I know nothin' of the sort," Link contradicted just as hotly. "They don't know it's the law that's up here! Come daylight, I'll have a word with 'em. Mebbe nothin' will come of it; but it won't cost nothin' to try. We better drop back before the rest of this outfit moves into range and gits its pants shot off."

He led them back the way he had come, and in a few minutes they met the rest of the posse. Now that he knew where to look for the enemy, Link proposed quitting the rim and in the few minutes of darkness left, taking up a position along the edge of the timber that would command the recently built road up the west wall of the canyon.

That was accomplished but not without bursts of gunfire from out on the rim. They were wild, searching shots that did no damage.

"They know we're gittin' set for tomorrow and they're tryin' to locate us," Grumpy muttered as he got down behind the trunk of a fallen pine, with Rainbow, Bent and half a dozen others.

"They'll be sorry they ever let us get in here," said Rip. "We'll be able to keep them from using the road, and we're high enough at the same time to break up any big move they try on the rim."

The tips of the high peaks to the east began to glow with the golden light of coming day some minutes before sun lifted its round face above the horizon. The harsh, unflattering dawn light revealed the preparations MacDonald's men had made for battle. On the rim itself, they had gathered up loose rock and erected a barricade several feet high. Rip took it for granted that it was from there the shots had come that had been fired at him and at Corbett.

How many men were stationed behind the barricade was a matter of speculation; but judging by the number concentrated on the slope, they were no mere handful. No one was to be seen on the road. In building it, however, huge blocks of granite had been dragged aside. It made an excellent breastwork. Behind it, running down from the scene of the blasting to within a few yards of the tie spur, Ambrose MacDonald had placed the bulk of his little army of construction workers. Up and down that line, wherever they looked, the partners caught the glint of sunlight on rifle barrels.

"By grab, he's armed every man Jack of 'em, as you purdicted, Rip," Grumpy commented soberly. "I don't know what kinda gunfighters his pick and shovel men will make, but it's a cinch they won't be pushed into the river without puttin' up a scrap."

"They'll give us all the fight we want," Rip said, his glance roving over the rim. "Shag will see to that. If he's bossing this business for MacDonald, Link will have to do his talking to him, and he'll get exactly nowheres . . . There he goes, holding a handkerchief up on a stick."

Link no sooner stepped out in the open than guns bristled along the rock barricade, out on the rim. Though he received no indication that his white flag would be respected, he did not hold back. Limping a little, he marched out until he was within speaking distance of the men who had their guns trained on him. It took courage, but that was something he had never lacked.

Raising his voice, he called out: "Can you hear me?"

"We hear you!" Shag answered. "But we ain't listenin' to anythin' from you!"

"This is the law speakin'!" Link warned. "Every man with me has been legally deputized! I'm givin' you fellas ten minutes to git off this rim and the slope! I'm takin' over till the Denver and Pacific can satisfy me that no more innocent people are goin' to be killed, or other folks' property destroyed, by its blastin' operations!"

"To hell with you and yore deputies!" Shag cried defiantly. "When you get ready to push us off of here—go to it!"

Link said no more. With his bony shoulders squared angrily, he turned on his heels and strode back to the timber. Rip and Grumpy were surprised that he reached it alive. He made his way along the line to them.

"You heard the answer I got," he ground out savagely. "Now they'll git mine."

"What do you propose to do?" Rip asked.

"We'll leave Dutch and a few men here so as not to give our play away; the rest of us will drop down to the bottom of the slope and go after those gents from the river side. We could throw lead at 'em all day from here and it wouldn't smoke 'em out."

"That'll be costly, Link," Rainbow declared soberly, though he had to agree that nothing could be accomplished from their present position. "They've got us outnumbered better than two to one. We'll be fighting uphill, and that always gives the other side the advantage."

"We'll try it, jest the same." The old man was in no mood to argue the matter. "You can't allus fight on yore terms."

It took the posse an hour to work down through the trees and get across the tie spur. Whoever was giving the orders to MacDonald's men surmised the purpose of the move and wasted a tremendous amount of ammunition in a vain attempt to stop it.

When the posse suddenly broke through to the river, there was a mad scrambling on the slope. MacDonald had stationed fully a hundred armed workmen there to guard the approach to the ledge and the rim above. Caught from the rear now, they had only to crawl over to the other side of the rocks and boulders to be in as good a position as ever. For a moment or two they were exposed, however. The valley men didn't wait for any word from Link. Whipping up their rifles, they spattered the side of the road with a sputtering, scattered fusillade. It cleared the slope in a hurry.

"By gum, they's a couple of them gents won't do no more fightin' for a day or two!" the sheriff cried. "There's Dutch openin' up on 'em!"

In scurrying around the rocks to get out of the line of fire from below, the defenders had left themselves open to attack from Dutch and the handful of men who had been left in the timber. All they could do now was to burrow down and hastily push up a low barricade of rocks. Safe temporarily, they began firing at the posse. The latter had no choice but to seek cover, too. Suddenly, the morning was still again; the action had not lasted more than three or four minutes, at most.

Link conferred briefly with the partners and Corbett. One of Uncle Joe's punchers was down, but not seriously injured.

"We can roll 'em up the slope if we go at 'em Injun fashion," the sheriff asserted grimly. "Don't let up on 'em now, boys! Pick yore rock and move up a foot or two at a time!"

He dispatched a messenger to inform Dutch of what they were going to do.

"You tell that crazy Dutchman to be careful or he'll be cuttin' us down."

Link's strategy succeeded for a time. The fight moved a third of the way up the slope, with the valley men getting the better of it. From the rim, Kissick and his gunmen fired methodically, their long-range slugs laying their hot breath on Rip and several others but finding no target. The little one crawled up beside Rainbow.

"We've come as far as we're goin'," he growled softly. "Look ahead! Not so much as a clump of sage for thirty yards!"

Even along the road there was no cover here. The terrain dipped and the hollow had been filled in. The defenders had retreated smartly and were now in position to resist further attack. Out on the fill they had left one of their number. The lumpy body lay there, face buried in the dust.

Save for an occasional shot, the fighting ceased. Link crawled up and looked the situation over. Overriding the partners' objections, he spread his men out so that they formed almost a quarter-circle and ordered them to advance.

The first rush was stopped before it got halfway across. Two men went down, both seriously wounded. A second attempt was equally unsuccessful.

"It won't work," Rainbow said flatly. "We'll be cut to pieces if you keep this up, Link. Give me an hour and four or five men and I'll get up on the rim of the east wall. There's no other way to win this fight."

The towering east wall of the canyon was high enough to command the slope and every inch of the opposite rim.

"What makes you think you can git up there?" the old man snapped.

"Bent says he knows the way. MacDonald may have the trail blocked. He can't have many men over there. I figure we can either go through them or slip past."

The sheriff thought it over for a few moments.

"Okay!" he decided. "Pick yore men."

"I'll take Grump, Bent and a couple of his C Bar boys. Bannon and Failes will do. You keep banging away, Link. Don't let that bunch get the idea you've changed your mind about storming up the slope."

As the crow flies, it was not more than two hundred yards from where Rainbow stood to the rim of the east wall. To reach it, however, Bent led them north through the San Cristobal hills, crossed the tie spur and swung far out in Painted Meadows to avoid the camp and reach Moran Mountain from the east. With due regard to the fact that they might ride into an ambush at any turning of the trail, they pressed forward and made the steep ascent unopposed.

The desultory gunfire from beyond the river swelled as they left their broncs in the cedars and crossed the rim on foot.

"By damn, we'll make short work of this!" Grumpy rapped, as the scene below unrolled. "Jest flatten down and begin throwin' lead!"

Bent glanced at Rainbow for confirmation.

"That's why we're here," the tall man said simply. "We're calling the tune at last. Let Kissick know what time it is, Grump."

Shag and his gunmen were stretched out on the rim at the head of the slope and firing an occasional shot at the posse. Grumpy's first slug was a trifle wide, but the spurt of dust it kicked up had an electric effect on them. Shag reared up on an elbow and flicked a quick glance at the opposite rim. His personal safety came first with him, but whatever his shortcomings, he was not a complete coward. With stark clarity, he realized that it was not only death to remain where he was but that the fight was lost unless whoever was on the east rim was quickly driven off.

Barking an order at his men, he leaped to his feet and, big and clumsy though he was, outdistanced them in a mad dash to the timber. Not all of them made it.

"I dropped one of 'em!" Bib Failes growled. "He ain't gittin' up!"

A second man staggered out of range.

"I was holdin' too high," Grumpy complained. "Musta been a shoulder hit. That's yore hired gunslingers for you! They'll run every time when the chips are down!"

The posse's horses were in the timber. Before the two men who were in charge of them knew what was happening, Shag and his gang swarmed over them, took the broncs they needed and were pounding downhill, leaving their wounded to shift for themselves. Ten minutes later, they flashed across the T. R. and N. tracks. There was no reason for them to avoid the camp. Racing through it, they drove up the mountain.

Unaware of what was happening, the partners turned their attention to the slope. MacDonald's men, caught from front and rear now, began to waver. A man threw his gun away. Another followed his example. Several jumped up, hands raised. It was the beginning of the end. In another minute or two, the fight was over.

From their perch on the east rim, Rainbow and the others saw the possemen disarming the construction crew and driving them back to camp.

"That does it," said Rip. "If Link can only hold fast there for five or six days, the Denver and Pacific will meet our terms."

"There's another 'if' connected with that, ain't there?" the little one queried.

"Yes, there is," Rainbow admitted, knowing Grumpy had reference to Moulton's coming. "But five or six days should give us time enough."

CHAPTER 21

RAINBOW AND the others got in the saddle and were about to leave the rim, when they noticed a moving plume of smoke in the direction of Lively.

"No mystery about that," Grumpy declared. "That's Con, on Number 3. I thought you told him to keep out of this, Rip."

"I did," the tall man grinned. "His curiosity got the better of him, I suppose. I'm not going to be annoyed over it; telling him to keep out of this fight was asking a lot."

They caught sight of the locomotive a minute or two later. Con ran down to within several hundred yards of the Y and stopped. A score of armed men jumped down from the tender and cab.

"There's reinforcements for you, Rip," Chick Bannon remarked, with an amused chuckle. "They seem to have got here a little too late."

"I don't know about that," Rainbow returned. "Link may be able to use them. He'll have to make some arrangements to keep himself supplied with men; most of the crowd that

came down with us last night won't be able to stick it out
for five or six days."

"He can rotate 'em," said Grumpy. "He can let boys like
Chick and Bib, here, go back to the ranch for twenty-four
hours and then come down again."

"That's what I meant," Rainbow said. "We can run down
grub and blankets by train . . . Suppose we get going."

All unsuspicious of what the next few minutes were to
bring, they began moving down the trail. Believing the fighting was over, they rode with their rifles in the saddle boots.

Grumpy ranged ahead. Though he was both hungry and
weary, it was characteristic of him that he was never completely off guard when in the saddle. It saved them now,
though if he had been exercising his usual caution he would
have caught the running of ponies long before he did. When
it finally rang a warning bell in his brain, he pulled up abruptly
and threw up a hand for Rip and the rest to stop.

"Listen!" came from him in a sharp, low cry.

The tall man caught the drumming of shod hoofs.

"We've got company! Get off the trail!"

Grumpy stood up in his stirrups, peering down the mountain. Six riders flashed into view and disappeared as quickly
around a turn. The little one swung back.

"It's Kissick's bunch, boys! Six of 'em! They'll be pilin'
into us in a minute or two!"

"Let them come," Rainbow said tightly. "We'll give them
a surprise. Don't bother with the rifles; use your belt guns."

"If we git the jump on 'em, they won't put up a fight!
What I said about hired gunslingers still goes! I never met
one yet that didn't turn yellow when you stuck a gun in his
belly."

The ominous quiet across the river had not gone unnoticed
by Shag and his followers. They drew from it the obvious
conclusion that the fighting was over. That it had gone against
their side was equally obvious. When some of his men suggested that they turn back, Shag would not listen. He had
fared badly at the hands of the partners from the start. It gave
him a personal score to settle. The chance that he would find

Rip and Grumpy among those on the east rim was enough to drive him on.

The trail grew steeper. It slowed their horses to a walk. They reached the head of that mean stretch and pulled up to blow the animals. Their surprise was complete when they suddenly found themselves hemmed in from right and left.

"Stick up your hands!" Rip droned.

The two riders in the lead broke down the trail in headlong flight. Grumpy blocked others from doing the same.

The upness of the jig was plain enough to Shag's cohorts. They stuck up their hands. He started to follow their example. But then, face to face with Rip, he froze for a split second and the hatred pounding through his brain swept all reason out of him. His hand slapped his holster, and he fired almost as soon as he had the gun out of the leather.

No wizard with a .44 under the best of circumstances, Shag's wild, hurried shot did not come within an arm's length of Rainbow, but in missing him, the slug tore into Bent Curry and buried itself deep beneath his heart.

Grumpy was out of position to do anything about it. Rip and Bib Failes whipped up their guns, but they were a moment too late. Chick Bannon, closer to Bent in many ways than the boy's father had been, snuffed the life out of Shag Kissick before they could fire.

That wasn't enough for Bannon—not when he saw Bent lose his grip on his saddlehorn and tumble limply to the ground. He had four cartridges left in his gun. He squeezed the trigger again and again.

Panic seized the three men who had ridden with Shag, and they were ready to break away, whatever the cost.

"Steady!" Rip warned. "If you want to get out of this with a whole hide, keep reaching!...Grumpy, you and Bib get their guns. Chase them down the mountain, then. If they don't move fast enough for you, bust 'em!"

Bannon had dropped to his knees beside Bent. Rainbow sat where he was, his gun ready, until Shag's men were run off. His face was rocky as he slipped out of the saddle and joined Bannon.

"He's breathin'," Chick got out tensely. "And he ain't bleedin' much. That could be a good sign, Rip. The slug may have just struck a rib and glanced off in back without hittin' anythin' vital."

"I hope so!" Rainbow said fervently. "I hope so! This is the one thing I didn't want to have happen, Chick. We went into this trouble on Jeannie's account. If she lose Bent, it won't matter much to her whether we win out or lose . . . Here's Grumpy and Bib."

"How bad did he git it?" the little one demanded anxiously.

"We can't say," Rainbow answered. "We'll have to carry him down the mountain. Thank God, we've got Con waiting for us! It may make all the difference in the world to this boy!"

"I'll carry him down," Bannon offered. "I carried him when he was a kid; I guess I can do it now." He rolled Kissick off the trail with his boot. "Christ, why wasn't I a second quicker?"

They lifted Bent up to Bannon without stirring a flicker of returning consciousness in him. That done, Rip told Grumpy and Bib to get down to Con and have him ready for a quick run to town.

"Chick and I will have to take it easy," he called to them as they swung away. "We'll be down as quickly as we dare."

He picked up the captured guns and tossed them in among the trees. In a few seconds, they began a careful descent of the mountain. When they reached the valley floor, they cut across to the T. R. and N. tracks in plain view of the camp but without interference.

Marcus Curry was among those who had come down on Number 3. Grumpy had given him word about Bent. Con had run down to the Y and turned the engine. While willing hands placed the boy on the floor of the cab, Rip called the little one aside.

"I want you to stay here, Grump. Take these men up the slope and find Link. I'll be down later in the day with grub and blankets. You know what to tell him. My advice would be to block the approach to the slope. If MacDonald makes another move, you can stop him before he gets started."

"I'll take care of everythin'," Grumpy assured him. "You have got the hard job, facing Jeannie."

Bent hovered between life and death for twenty-four hours as he lay in Doc Trombly's house. Lively had no hospital. Rip suggested having a train made ready that Bent might be taken to White River Junction.

"They couldn't do anything for him down there that I can't do here," Trombly objected. "Mark wants the boy taken home. I won't consent to that either. I've located the slug. It traveled along the rib and lodged against the spine. Naturally, it's produced a paralysis. I believe he'll come back quickly, as soon as the slug is removed."

It was late in the afternoon of the second day before Bent was pronounced out of danger. Jeannie was permitted to see him for a few minutes. It had been an ordeal for her. Now that it was over, Rip could see that she was near to collapse. He insisted that she keep away from the depot.

"I want you to go to bed and stay there for a day or so," he told her. "Con's replaced several damaged rails in the canyon. There doesn't seem to be any reason why we should not resume service in the morning. We can't handle the wire. Otherwise, we'll manage without you, Jeannie."

"And you really believe we've got them licked, Rip?"

"I wouldn't go that far," he answered, with a smile. "But some signs point to it. MacDonald isn't doing any work. The ties we're delivering at Chipeta are piling up. I expected the Denver and Pacific to start some legal move to have Link ousted. But they haven't. Link's given me his word he'll hold fast till he's satisfied there'll be no more trouble down there."

"It all sounds encouraging, Rainbow. I haven't been able to think for a day or two . . . Everyone's been so kind to me— even Mr. Curry."

"You get some sleep," the tall man urged. "Don't come back on the job till you feel able."

With Bent on the mend and two others who had suffered

serious injury doing well, Rip could say that his side had not lost a man. MacDonald had not been as fortunate. Counting Shag Kissick, three of his men had been killed and so many wounded that he had sent over Mears Pass and brought in a railroad doctor from Middle Park.

Lem Spade rode up to the depot about five o'clock. Rip was alone in the office.

"I've caught up on a few things," Lem told him. "I'm goin' down and spend a day or two with Link. Any word you want to send him or yore pardner?"

"Yeh. You can tell them we're resuming service in the morning."

Lem nodded. "That's good news. By the way, Rip, are you goin' to try to collect damages from the D. and P. over the blastin'?"

"I figure that would be a waste of time and money. Why do you ask, Lem?"

"Wal, Warren and me figgered he had a suit ag'in 'em— 'Liza killed and the young 'un hurt. We saw Purcell this afternoon. He says to forget it; that we'd have to prove the charge that did the damage didn't go off accidental."

"I'm afraid you'd be suing them forever and get little in the end," said Rainbow. "I can't promise you anything, but I'll say this: if we make a deal with the D. and P. I'll see that they take care of Warren."

Con came in soon after Spade left. Rainbow spoke to him about sending the morning train out on schedule.

"Shure and I don't see how she'll get into the depot down there if we can't use the wire and let thim know whin she's due," Con protested. "We have to cross their tracks. There's a derailer. They keep it open till the tower gives us the highball to come in."

"I'm aware of all that, Con. But can't Pop hoof it into the tower?"

Hanrahan rubbed his long shrewd nose.

"That he can do," he admitted reluctantly. "I wouldn't call it railroading. I can imagine what Pop will call it."

"It will only be for a day or two," said Rip. "You notify

Pop and the rest of the crew to be ready to pull out on time in the morning."

That makeshift arrangement was carried out until Jeannie was back on the job. It served its purpose as far as Bannerman and the other Lively merchants were concerned. The road's passenger business, light at any time, seemed to have disappeared altogether. The only way Rainbow could account for it was the men and women were fearful that the disaster that had snuffed out Eliza Warren's life might be repeated. The lack of business was not important; he was waiting for Henry Moulton.

On the evening of Jeannie's return to the office, Rip was on the platform when the up train pulled in. Four men got down from the coach. One was a smooth-shaven, ruddy-faced man of fifty. He had the unstudied air of importance about him that successful executives of big corporations seem to acquire with the years. Instinctively, Rip knew that the man was Moulton. The latter's sense of perception was equally keen.

"I'm sorry I couldn't get here sooner," Moulton remarked, as they shook hands. "I've heard about you and your partner so many times it's like meeting an old acquaintance. I knew you at first glance, Ripley. I want you to meet these gentlemen. I brought them down from Cheyenne. This is Tom Bradley. Tom's been with us for years. When we have a tough engineering problem to crack, we turn it over to him. This is Bob Searles and Dick Graney, from Tom's department. I thought as long as I was here to twist Ambrose MacDonald's tail I'd come prepared to give it a good twist."

"He knows you, of course," said Rip. "How about the rest?"

"He's acquainted with Tom," Moulton answered. "These youngsters are strangers to him. I understand we are to give the impression that we don't want MacDonald to know we're here."

"I think that will help," Rainbow told him, his gray eyes twinkling. "I'll take you up to the hotel. When you register, I'd suggest that you and Mr. Bradley not use your right names.

MacDonald has spies in town. You won't be here long before he knows it. When he looks at the register and finds you are using aliases, it should go a long way toward convincing him that you have some plans afoot."

Moulton and Bradley joined in a hearty laugh.

"This is going to be fun," Moulton told the tall man. "We're putting ourselves in your hands. The boys know what the game is. They won't let the cat out of the bag."

Grumpy came up that night to find Moulton and Bradley upstairs with Rip, who was giving them an account of the fight and the situation in general. The little one's skepticism faded as the discussion continued and Moulton made some suggestions for the morrow.

"It sounds fine to me," Grumpy declared. "I jest wonder if they don't know already that yo're here."

"We didn't advertise it," Moulton told him. "We reached White River Junction over the Midland, and we didn't come by private car. I know what we'd do if we were actually interested in buying the property. If we proceed along those lines, little Ambrose will take the bait."

It was late before their guests went to their rooms.

"We couldn't ask no more of them," Rip remarked with enthusiasm as soon as he and the little man were alone.

"I agree with that, Rip," Grumpy was unduly sober. "What I want to know is what yo're goin' to tell Jeannie."

"Only what I've already told her. I went back to the depot and spent a few minutes with her and Con while Moulton's party was getting settled. I said nothing about the Union Pacific. I told them Moulton was interested in looking the road over but that we were not at liberty to say who he represented. I warned them not to say anything and they gave me their word they wouldn't."

"Okay," the little man muttered. "That makes me feel better!"

CHAPTER 22

RIP WAS AT the depot early and instructed Con to have Number 3 and a day coach ready to run down to the canyon, after the morning train departed. Searles and Graney, the young civil engineers, appeared soon after and in the baggage room opened the specially designed trunk that had accompanied them and got out a transit and the other tools of their profession.

Grumpy arrived with Moulton and Bradley as the down train was pulling out. A few minutes later, the little party left to spend the day in Ute Canyon. To make certain that they would be watched, they got off at Chipeta and proceeded on foot, with Number 3 following them.

For several hours they moved up and down the canyon, with Bradley making notes of the contours and width of the roadbed. For good measure, he had the surveyors run some imaginary levels. Ambrose MacDonald's abortive attempt to blast a roadbed out of the west wall amused him, as it did Moulton.

"Ambrose figures you are greenhorns, or he wouldn't have

tried such a preposterous bluff on you," said the latter. "If he had a roadbed up there, what good would it do him? A snowslide would pluck off a train and send it crashing into the river. If he built snowsheds, they'd go down, too. I believe you've got him stymied."

As they suspected, MacDonald had his scouts watching every move they made. The suspicious nature of the party's activities was promptly reported to him. He chose to sit tight in his headquarters tent until Steve Lundy, head of construction, came in with the startling news that he had recognized Tom Bradley.

"There's no question about it, Boss," Lundy asserted. "I'd say the gent with him is Henry Moulton, no less; but of that I'm not sure."

MacDonald was now ready to see for himself. He was too late, however; Number 3 was steaming back to Lively. Determined to get to the bottom of it, he ordered his team hitched. An hour later, he drove into town and went to the hotel at once. The names he looked for did not appear on the register. He interrogated the clerk to no avail and then described Moulton.

"You must have the name wrong," the clerk informed him. "It's Mr. Martin you want. I believe you can find him down at the depot or north of town. The whole party was up there a short time ago with Rainbow and Grumpy." Enjoying MacDonald's chagrin, he added, "I hear they're getting ready to survey a railroad up through Painted Meadows."

MacDonald could not dissemble his anxiety. He supplied his own answer to all this secrecy. Hurrying out to his rig, he glanced down the street and saw Rainbow coming up the sidewalk with Moulton and Bradley. He recognized all three immediately. Turning his team in the other direction, he drove out of town at a furious clip.

Completely taken in by the ruse, his first thought was to get in touch with Alvin Ketchel at once. He couldn't use the Thunder River and Northern's wire. It left him nothing to do but send a rider post-haste over Mears Pass into Middle Park, where the D. and P. had established telegraphic connection with Denver.

The hotel clerk called Moulton and Rip over to the desk and gave them an account of what had passed between Ambrose MacDonald and himself.

"He asked for a Mr. Moulton, but he was looking for you, Mr. Martin. He turned green when I told him you had your surveyors working north of town. I don't see how you missed him; he busted out of here just a minute before you stepped in."

"I thought I saw him drive away," Rip said, with a poker face. "We'll be upstairs if he comes back."

Moulton and he exchanged a knowing grin as they turned away.

"He's hooked, Rip! He saw us and he couldn't get away fast enough. He'll lose no time getting in touch with the general offices in Denver. The next thing you know, you'll see Ketchel out here again."

"I hope you're right," Rainbow told him. "I'm glad you and Bradley are going to be with us another day."

"It wouldn't look right to Ambrose if we stayed longer. We'll leave Searles and young Graney here till the break comes. They can go on running levels and sawing wood."

Moulton and Bradley left on Thursday morning. The partners saw them off. Nothing further had been heard from MacDonald.

It was a long, hard day for Rip and Grumpy. It was not easy to pretend that everything was all right, especially to Jeannie, when the outcome was still as much a matter of speculation as ever. That evening, however, Ambrose MacDonald arrived at the depot and paced the platform, obviously waiting for the up train. When it pulled in, the first man down the steps was Alvin Ketchel.

"We got 'em!" Grumpy jerked out under his breath. "Moulton called the turn!"

Ketchel saw them and after conferring briefly with MacDonald walked over.

"You remember me, of course," he began.

"Certainly," Rainbow acknowledged.

"And you're acquainted with Mr. MacDonald. I'm here to do business with the two of you."

"No hurry about it," said Rip.

"We think there is. You're making this thing so costly for us, Ripley, that we've decided to accept your terms."

"What terms?" the tall man queried with little show of interest.

"Well!" Ketchel exclaimed with some annoyance. "I thought the terms were clearly understood." He glanced at Mac-Donald. "I was told you insisted that after we came over Mears Pass that we follow the old Ute trail and cut down to Lively and strike out for the canyon from here."

"That's correct—if the price is," Rainbow said coolly.

"The price is a hundred thousand dollars," MacDonald spoke up. The tall man shook his head.

"We have a better offer, gentlemen."

"Have you made any commitment?" Ketchel inquired, after studying him for a moment.

"We haven't signed any papers."

"Then suppose you name your figure," the lawyer snapped back.

"We ain't puttin' a price on the road," Grumpy interjected. "We'll listen to any proposition you care to make. If it suits us, we'll do business."

"You've got to consider the money we've spent at Chipeta," said Ketchel. "It'll be a dead loss to us . . . Will you take a hundred and fifty thousand?"

It was as much as Rip expected to get. Instead of grabbing it, he pretended to be undecided.

"I think we can get more by waiting, Mr. Ketchel. If you want to leave the offer open for a few days, we'll think it over."

Discarding his usual suavity, Ketchel said, "Ripley, I've got a preliminary agreement in my briefcase, with the proper signatures affixed. I am ready to fill in the figure and hand you the contract, together with a certified check for fifty thousand, the balance to be payable on the signing of the final papers, if you'll take a hundred and seventy-five thousand. It obligates us to use the Ute trail-Lively route. You can have your lawyer look it over before you sign."

It was a far greater sum of money than Rainbow had ever dealt for, though his manner did not hint that such was the case. He mentioned the Warren matter.

"The mother was killed, her daughter injured. I figure the father is entitled to damages to the extent of ten thousand dollars.

"We won't quibble about it," Ketchel assured him. "I don't want to incorporate it in the contract, but you have my word that we'll take care of it."

"All right," Rip announced, "the Thunder River and Northern is yours—if the papers are in order."

"I believe you will find that to be the case," Ketchel's tone was crisp and sharp. Opening his briefcase, he produced the agreement and filled in the figure with his fountain pen.

"Will you look me up at the hotel this evening?" he inquired, as he handed the documents to Rainbow.

"Sometime after supper," Rip replied.

Jeannie couldn't believe the good news at first.

"What about those gentlemen who were here the other day, Rainbow?"

"Jeannie—you've got to keep mum about this for the present. It was a hoax—something we arranged." He tapped the papers Ketchel had given him. "This was what we were after."

Her knees felt weak and she had to sit down.

"A hundred and seventy-five thousand for the T. R. and N. Think of it! There's been times when I didn't know where the next meal was coming from."

"That'll never happen ag'in," Grumpy assured her. "Rip and me went into this fight for only two reasons; to git you a square deal and keep Lively on the map. We decided long ago that if we made any money half of it was yores."

"Oh, no!" she protested. "I can't take it! You're too generous."

"We won't have any argument about that," Rip said firmly. "Put on your hat and we'll walk over and tell Bent the good news!"

Jeannie felt she was walking on air as she tripped along with them.

"Wait until tonight!" she said. "The town will go wild when the good news gets around."

"By grab, that's somethin' I want to see!" the little one declared happily. "I hope I'm called on to make a speech. I've had one prepared for weeks. Jest two lines: Hooray for Lively! May she be lively once more!"

Renegade by Ramsay Thorne

WARNER BOOKS
P.O. Box 690
New York, N.Y. 10019

Please send me the books I have checked. I enclose a check or money order
(not cash), plus 50¢ per order and 50¢ per copy to cover postage and handling.*
(Allow 4 weeks for delivery.)

_____ Please send me your free mail order catalog. (If ordering only the
catalog, include a large self-addressed, stamped envelope.)

Name _____

Address _____

City _____

State _____ Zip _____

*N.Y. State and California residents add applicable sales tax.   11

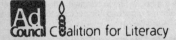